WHEN THE WALLS HAVE EARS

SHABU KILITHATTIL

TRANSLATED BY
DR. JAYA ANITHA ABRAHAM

GULF BOOK
SERVICES

Published By:	**Gulf Book Services Ltd,**
	20-22 Wenlock Road, London.
	NI 7GU
	UK
	Email: info@gulfbooks.co.uk

ISBN: 978-1-7392159-9-6
Year: November 2023

GULF BOOK
SERVICES

Shabu Kilithattil

Born in Puravoor, Chirayeenkeezhu in Thiruvananthapuram district.Postgraduate diploma in journalism from the Institute of Journalism, Thiruvananthapuram Press Club.

Worked at Mathrubhumi and Akashavani. Also worked on the editorial board of "Shasthra kauthukam" 'programme prepared by C- DIT for Doordarshan. Since 2004, he is the news director of Hit 96.7FM of the Arabian Radio Network in Dubai.

His other published books include Yadhardha Pavakalikkaar, Sarga Srishtiyile Raasavidyakal, Mariya Gulfum Gafoorka Dosthum, Special News, Nilachoru, Kalam Kavalam, Mazha Mannu Manushyan and Randu Neela Malsyangal. He also wrote dialogues for the film 'Angels' and directed a documentary on Rangaprabhath, a theatre initiative for children.

He has received numerous awards including the Parappurathu Award for short stories, the Kairali Award for novels, the Saparya Literary Award, the Sarga Sameeksha Award of the Pravasi Book Trust, the inaugural Kavalam Narayana Panikkar Foundation Literary Award, 2022 India Press Club of North America Exemplary Radio Journalism Award, Sharjah India Association Media Award, Green Voice Media Award, C P Sreedharan, M N Viyyoth, Sharidaya Padiyath, Chiranthana, Asia Vision etc.,

He was also awarded the UAE Golden Visa in recognition of his services to the media sector.

Wife: Anasooya, Children: Jahnav, Sreehari
E mail: shabuarn@gmail.com

Dr. Jaya Anitha Abraham

Born in the district of Pathanamthitta.
Doctorate in Economics from Mahatma Gandhi University.
Worked in Kerala Horticulture Development Programme
(KHDP), IIM-K and ICFAI. She has been teaching
Economics and Statistics at Abu Dhabi University since
2011. She has received academic fellowships from the
Indian Council of Agriculture Research and Indian Social
Science Research.
She is also a Fellow of the Academy of Higher Education.

She was awarded the UAE Golden Visa in recognition of
her achievements in the academia.

Her literary interests include writing and translating poetry.
She writes poetry as an expression of her reaction to the
world around her. Her work has been published in major
international online portals such as Modern Literature,
Literary Hatchet, Poetria, Mad Swirl, etc.

Husband: Shibu P Jacob Children: Deeya, Deepu
E mail: abrahamjaya@gmail.com

For the native tribes
In search of solace,
For the wandering children
In search of a rudder,
For the mother
Who sheltered…

The glowing embers of life
O V Usha

The Book of Life has a coarse, rabid script that hides in dark corners, never willing to grapple with language. The graph of life is so complex that we are unable to transcribe it perfectly. If anyone manages to write it at all, they must use the writing of reality- the blood itself. Then these words would enter the hearts of the readers like glowing coals. In the novel "When the Walls Have Ears" by Shabu Kilithattil, a scorching heat awaits the reader.

This novel passionately portrays the ethos of a young girl's life as she wanders alone through the dark forests of life, unaware of its lush greenery. It is a jungle filled with the maddening cries and sobs of a girl. The journey with this girl is a heartbreaking experience. But she proves to everyone that she magically conquers the wildness of the jungle.

Watch how quickly this innocent character, born and raised in humble circumstances, falls headlong into the vortex of brutality. Then she is chased through many worlds. We have realized countless times that our world is a theatre that oppresses the female spirit and bodies in its barbaric claws. This novel artistically renders the truths that exist around us.

There was no place of refuge from which she did not seek shelter. She even went to Calcutta to meet Mother Teresa, the angel of goodness and mercy. She was dragged both to the doors of the red street of Bombay and to the dark blue alleys of the tinsel world. Amazingly, she survived all this with the charisma of her soul. Though she took blows, she transformed herself into a great grove of kindness. With her bravery, she builds and maintains a paradise called Shanthi.

While reading this book, you would fervently pray for Uma, the main character of the story, at every moment.

Even as a toddler, she is thrust into the dangerous traps of life. She could never enjoy the love of a mother who shackled her with kindred love. When her mother left, she helped her father and younger brother with her little fingers. When she returned, she had become a pimp who bargained for Uma's youthful body. She went through countless tragedies of life. Along the way, she attains a level of lionheartedness that will astonish the reader. Her decision to donate her kidney to an unknown young man she met by chance in a hospital is a case in point.

The hurdles that come up in Uma's life make us anxious. But each chapter also reassures us out of these worries too. The narration is deft enough to bring the character of Uma into the hearts of the readers. Not only Uma, but all the characters will flash in our minds after reading.

This story is not a figment of imagination but merges with real life, honestly, strand by strand.

If you read this book without forgetting this fact, your heart will bleed every moment. This is reality; this is a novel that translates the silent, incessant cries between debacle and survival.

"When the walls have ears portrays my real life. Everything I have seen, heard and gone through"
-Uma Preman

Born 1970 in Coimbatore. Primary education in Coimbatore. Started Shanthi Medical Information Centre in Thrissur district by collecting all available medical information and travelling all over India. Donated a kidney in 1999.

Till date, nearly 200,000 dialyses, more than 100 medical camps, 680 kidney transplants and about 20500 heart surgeries have been performed under Shanthi's patronage.

She founded the Attappadi Tribal Welfare Project, a dialysis unit in Lakshadweep. She has received nearly 50 awards, including the Real Hero Award from CNN IBN (2010), the Asianet Sthree Shakthi Award (2014) and the Vanitha Woman of the Year Award (2015).

She founded APJ Abdul Kalam Tribal Residential School in Pattimalam, Attapadi to provide better education to tribal children without losing the tribal culture and values.

Her only son Sharat Sagar works as an Assistant Director, after completing his training in visual communication.

Preface

Uma Preman told me the poignant story of her life as we travelled by car from Thrissur to Attappadi. A story of loneliness and broken dreams straight from childhood. She carried the silent burden of pain and alienation she had experienced all her life.

During the journey, she told me how bleak her childhood and youth were, without even a drop of love, and how unexpected blows of fate hit her.

In the midst of her orphanhood, imposed on her by her own relatives, she had dreamed of an island of hope, but not even a ray of joy fell upon her. The heartbreaking story of how she toiled for others while the hot coals of darkness burned within her, saddened me.

Uma Preman founded Shanthi Gramam to wipe the tears of the neglected people of Palamala, Bhoothathan Kettu and Attappadi. She continues to work for the reconstruction and revival of the one-teacher schools in Attappadi to keep the dreams of the tribal children alive. She brings new light into the lives of the marginalized.

Thus, she tries to bury her dark past with a sacrificial present. This is not the sympathy of a person groping in the dark towards people with similar experiences.

Her life bears witness to the fact that her tenderness is innate.

Over time, she has recovered the vague memories that lay scattered in the mines of her past. I have presented them to the readers with creativity and humility.

To O V Usha, who wrote the foreword despite her illness and encouraged me with motherly affection...

To Mr Madhavan Menon and Gulf Book Services who agreed to publish this work.

To all the friends who stood by me.

To Mr Ramesh Periya for designing the cover page. To Mr Ashok Kumar and Kairali books for publishing Nilachoru in Malayalam.

To the light that illuminated my thoughts and the air that breathed new words into me on my writing journey...

Thank you...
Shabu Kilithattil

CONTENTS

It has been a long time since we started.

In the twilight it was difficult to walk along the hilly path. The path, which resembles life, had its ups and downs. For those who are used to walking on straight, clear paths, this is certainly unbearable.

The dense undergrowth guarded the ground and we tried to break through it to make progress.

It was an adventurous act.

I had no desire to turn back.

We went forward. Valli joined us, holding the torch.

Valli had done her best to convince us not to go searching at dusk. It was I who insisted.

We must find out. The darkness or other obstacles did not worry me.

Although it was early evening, it was pitch dark in the tribal settlements.

The shadows of the dark sky fell around.

The houses in the tribal colonies of Attappadi stand like fireplaces in a thinned bush.

Same size. Same shape. Although no people were moving, the sounds of goats and cows could be heard.

In most houses, the goats and cows were kept in makeshift rooms with sloping roofs attached to the outside walls of the houses. They did not even have the facilities of a cattle shed.

Yet it was a cattle shed. The animals eat and defecate there. With the heavy rain last night, all the dirt was spread out in the courtyard.

Stench. The stench is everywhere.

There is no point in blaming the cattle. People are also facing similar situations. No house has a toilet. When we first met, Mallippennu complained about this very thing.

'Ma'am, ee ooruthi oru koonuthume kakkoos illai,there orakkethe velikki pokaathu.Aaa thanniyeme kudikkithu.Ivaraarume soru soralla pannamaattaru.Vediyaale koorethu irunthu ponaakki anthiyodethe thrumbi koorekke vrukthe. Ivaaru alla government oro koore ketti koduthukkaru.Athu mannmu,karinkallkkme kettina koorakkathe athne avvaru odukku kathmille; osaarikathmilley......

Ma'am, there is no toilet in any house in this village. They relieve themselves on the riverbanks. They drink the same water. These people do not cook food. They go out in the morning and come back in the evening. The government has built houses for them out of mud and granite. They are not cleaned and not properly maintained. The goats, cows, dogs and chickens live in the same house."

I listened to Mallippennu, who continued to speak in a low voice. Her words had a certain rhythm. Most of these people spoke a language that was a mixture of Malayalam and Tamil. Although I did not understand many of her words, I understood what she was complaining about. Governments have implemented several projects to reduce malnutrition in tribal colonies. Mallippennu is the coordinator for one of these projects.

But she was sure that just announcing such projects is not enough to improve the lives of the tribals. The tribals do not lead a systematic life.

The sky above, earth below...

The mechanisms of the civilized world have never affected them. They live as they wish. It was my curiosity about such a person that led me to this late evening walk.

Since I arrived in Agali, Valli has helped me. She goes to the villages, gets to know the people and learns more details about them. She has completed Plus Two. She would like to continue her studies. But her situation is unfavourable.

After a long walk, we reached a small, dilapidated building with a single room near a stream. Nearby was a neglected well. On the roof of this room, some pieces of a fallen iron pipe and parts of a disused water tank lay as evidence of the past, waiting for someone.

As it had become dark, it was quite difficult to see anything. I looked around. Once it may have been a farm. The well and the pump house bore witness to that.

"Ma'am," Valli called me in a low voice. I turned and looked at her. She pointed her finger at the corner of the dilapidated one-room pump house. My eyes followed her finger.

It stopped at a narrow beam of light.

The light, coming from a beedi lit at one corner of a mouth.

Valli and I exchanged glances.

A kind of dejection enveloped us.

Without making a sound, I went there. Valli tried to stop me, but I ignored it. She too followed me.

As I approached the human figure sitting leaning against the wall of the pump house smoking a beedi, I felt nauseous from the oppressive smell emanating from her.

I covered my nose with the end of my saree. The person's face was unrecognizable in the darkness. But I recognized that she had a dirty figure with matted hair. I remembered the name Valli had given and called her in a low voice.

"Ponnee"

Again, the light of the beedi shone on her lips. In the glow I saw the expression in her eyes.

It was not fear.

Those two eyes sparkled at me. She took the beedi from her lips between the fingers of her right hand and stood up. Valli hid behind me, transfixed by her gaze.

I looked at her from head to toe.

A very fragile and thin body. To hide it, she wrapped a shabby sari around her body, full of dirt and dust. The smell of urine from the saree made me dizzy.

Valli pulled my hand and said it in a hushed tone.

"Ma'am....... *Vaa naam pokilaa, Ponni bhayangaramaayi panamkukku ketta vakkellaa solluka, naa me pokilaa.*

Madam, let us go. When she is angry, Ponni uses very dirty words. Let us go."

For this reason, Valli was afraid of Ponni. She uses bad words. When she is angry, she does anything. Valli wants to escape before Ponni uses swear words.

I have thought of a way to calm Ponni down. Calmly, with love in my voice, I called Ponni.

She stood there looking grim as if she could not hear me.

I bent down and tried to touch her hand. She shook herself and took a step back. When she saw that I was not backing away, she threw the almost burnt out beedi at me and shouted.

"*Meda lethaakoole neeyaru...enne letthakku nee aaru? Nee enna raaniyaa? Nee podee poonda makale...Aaraadee agalikku raaniyaa? Enne paakkaakku aaru ninakku adhikaara thanthaaru?*

Who are you to control me? Who are you to come close to me? Are you the queen? You bitch, get out of here... Are you the queen of Agali? Who gave you the right to come to me?"

The more vulgar her words became, the more Valli wanted to run away from there. She tried to pull me by force and run away. When I heard Ponni screaming, I too became alarmed. But as a last resort, I went forward and pulled Ponni by her sari. This brought out the worst in Ponni. She screamed at the top of her lungs and jumped towards me.

"Poonde makale, moonchikke kaakkirunthu thuppinaa..ninthenthu vendethu letthaa?

You bitch... I will spit in your face... What do you want?"

She was getting ready to attack me. Startled, Valli ran away. I followed her. I looked back as we reached a path lit by the streetlight. I saw Ponni chasing us, pulling her sari up to her knees. I thought it was useless to run away. I decided to confront her. I took a twig from the side of the path, gathered my courage and walked towards her.

Ponni controlled herself when she saw the stick in my hand. She squatted down on the ground. Like an obedient child, she looked at me quite pitiably. I picked her up and held her hand. A foul stench came up my nose as I held her, who had not bathed, washed or changed her clothes for a long time.

"Come, Ponni, you are my friend. Let me bathe you."

Without a word she looked woefully into my eyes. Valli was astonished. She was speechless when she saw that

Ponni, who usually behaved hysterically and hurled expletives at everyone, was submissive. I went and held her tightly even though she smelt of urine.

As I interlaced my hand with hers and held her, she looked at me intently.

I saw in her eyes a glimmer of relief and security which she perceived.

Ponni is the symbol of the abused tribal girls. My desire to meet Ponni grew as Valli told her story while delivering the news in the tribal settlements. She was pretty, fair, and slender in stature.

*"Ponneene Moolagangan Oorukkethe ponnuvittathu.Poka vare nalla irunthaa.Aangutha aalkalode senthu velekalkkum aadumaadu mekka poyimthe…......*Ponni was married to Moolagangan Ooru. She was doing well till then. Along with the people there, she went to work and grazed the sheep and cattle."

Valli only heard rumours about Ponni. She told them as if she had heard them first hand.

"Aadumaadu mekka poyimthe kanjavu sedika alla kandaa. Velakku pokaravalla valikkthe paathu ponnikkmu aase vanthathu.Mothalu irantha elakalkke vetth valthu kaattinaaru. Pinne thaathane beedikke valikka thodaakinaa. Pinne kanjaavillaathe avalukku irkaakku mudikaale.Aala satthathme ava Aglikke aa njdu thirunthu. Ruttume pakalume pakkamaa naddanthu vanthu senthaa. Appathe ava umbaa masaaru ketta mathiri aana. Pinne rottu rotta summa nadappa.avare ivare kaashu keppaa. Thuni aada maatta … Thuni nalla poda maatta .Chorum thanneemillathe rottithiye nadappaa.

As she was grazing the sheep, she came across the cannabis plant. She saw the workers smoking it and wanted to do the same. First, she rolled the leaves and smoked them. Then she started smoking the beedi. After some time, she could not do without the kick. When her husband passed away, she came back to Agali. Without paying attention to the time, she walked back to Agali. At that time, she was completely deranged. She wandered along the road. She begged for money. Sometimes without clothes or in shabby clothes. Hungry, she walks along the street. "

In tribal settlements, it is very common to marry off girls when they are very young. Ponni was also married off at the age of fifteen.

The following year she gave birth to a baby girl. According to Valli, she became addicted to alcohol and cannabis while doing odd jobs for her husband's people. Since then, no one has seen her without drinking toddy or smoking beedi.

It may be that in this way she found her safety. A girl like Ponni would have thought that living without caring for one's body was the way to go. Due to the excessive consumption of intoxicants, she became mentally unbalanced.

She stank both physically and mentally.

No one dared to go near her. That was how strong the stench emanating from her was. She endured it, and if anyone approached her, she flung the filth from her mind with swear words.

Everyone was afraid of Ponni.

It is the same Ponni who now walks obediently with me.

We took her to one of the washrooms that 'Shanthi' had built. She sat there with her head down. Valli came with soap and shampoo.

I took a cup full of water and poured it over Ponni's body. To apply the soap, I touched her on the back. With a hiss she jumped up. Angry and pointing her finger at me, she said,

"*Enne   aarum   thodandaa..enne   aarum
thanneelattavaandaa..ekku   odambe   thoduvathu   ekku
pudikkathu….* No one needs to touch me. No one needs to
bathe me. I do not like anyone to touch me. "

She does not want anyone to touch her. I was taken
aback by her words. Had everyone declared this woman
crazy? Was she just pretending? Did she think that to
protect herself from the crazy world, it was better to act
crazy? A flood of questions rushed through my mind.

She is still resisting. Similar to her previous behaviour.

She is still angry.

"No, Ponni. You wash yourself. I will not touch you.
Pour water, apply soap and take a bath."

After the bath she shivered, for her body had not been
wet for several months. She thought there were no other
clothes. So she tried to wrap the old, dirty saree around
herself again. I took it off her and threw it away.

"Do not wear it again. I will give you a good one."

I said with a smile. "Ponni, are we not friends?"

Washing with soap and water drastically changed Ponni's
appearance. As the dirt and mud fell off her, the wild look
disappeared.

She is really beautiful. I gave her my saree that I had
brought for the next day and a shirt. She wore it. I saw a
faint smile on her face as she wore the new clothes. She was
babbling like a child.

"Chechy, buy me parotta. Chechy, tea too. Tobacco and
betel leaves for mother. Bangles and necklaces for
Lakshmi... Chechy, give me money."

She asks me to buy tobacco and betel leaves for her
mother and bangles and a necklace for her daughter. What
is she not aware of?

Who says she is crazy? I felt sorry for her. I held her
tightly and kept walking. To Sharavanan's tea shop...

After drinking tea and parotta, she held on to my arm and walked on. She looks transformed. Valli is still amazed. The twinkle in her eyes told me that this was not Ponni, whom she had known for years.

"Ponni."

With my hands on her shoulder, I called her affectionately. She answered me. I stroked my hand over her matted hair and asked,

"Your hair is messy. Shall we cut it?"

She looked at me and nodded in agreement. She looked younger as her matted hair and dirt were gone.

She looked prettier. Seeing her clearly, I shuddered. A shudder of fear. Was not I supposed to be comforted by the transformation of a woman who, with her foul stench and fierce appearance, was trying to keep herself safe from the claws of wild dogs?

But how?

I felt unusually anxious as I thought about how I could create a safe haven for her.

I took her in my arms and said,

"Ponni, you must take a bath every day. Change your clothes too. Do you hear?

I left some clothes with Valli to change into. Not only you. You have to keep your house clean too."

Ponni looked at me silently.

The construction of toilets in the tribal colonies is in its final stages. Along with the toilets, we also built a temporary rest house for nearly twenty families in Kandiyoor. Two nurses from Shanthi were there. Bindu and Malli made sure that the houses were cleaned, that the sick received medicine in time and that nutritious food was cooked for the children and pregnant women. In the evenings, the centre became very active.

They chatted for a while over tea and biscuits and then went home late in the evening. We also organized private tuition for the students there.

So, there was a noticeable change in the people. They became aware of keeping themselves, their houses and their surroundings clean and neat.

Ponni amazed everyone. Ponni took a bath daily, appeared clean and behaved politely. When she came to the rest home in the evening, she brought a glass with her. I was amazed at Ponni drinking tea in her glass only because she didn't like drinking from a glass that someone else had used.

When I reach the tribal colony, she'll join me. Although she doesn't talk much, she nods. Sometimes she even smiles. Although she had promised never to use cannabis or alcohol, she occasionally broke that promise. She took great pains to hide it from me.

Whenever I found out about it, I reprimanded her sternly. This might have frightened her.

On that particular day, it was similar. I scolded her when I came to know that she was smoking a cannabis beedi that someone had given her.

Without making any reply, she kept listening. Nowadays she behaves like that. She understands that she did wrong. Seeing her pitiful look, I took her to Sharavanan's tea shop.

That evening, the sky was dark and the clouds threatened to rain.

She had her eyes fixed on me as she took parotta and tea.
"What's wrong, Ponni?"
I repeated my question.
"What's the matter? Why are you staring at me like that?
With a smile, she replied.

"Nenakku masaaru thane ....enne pakkaakku nee enaakku varuthaa nee aaru?

Aren't you crazy to come and take care of me? Who are you?"

I didn't understand what she was saying and looked at Valli seeking help. She burst out laughing and covered her mouth.

"Tell me, what did Ponni say?" I pressed on.

That you were crazy, ma'am!"

My eyes bulged and I looked at Ponni. She nodded again.

"*Enne ella nalla pannu kaakka vanthaare-nenkkumaasaaruthen....* You came to protect me and take care of me. You must be mad."

She showed her discoloured teeth and laughed. I too laughed heartily.

The rain came with a roar and pelted down in buckets.

PART 1
CHILDHOOD
Pure Water

ONE

"Do not touch me. Do not touch me with the hands that touch the old women. I feel bad. "

I brushed my father's hand away as he tried to help me get out of the horse carriage. He looked at me without a word and walked in front of me. We did not speak to each other until we reached the bus stop. Every now and then he would turn and look at me. To see if I was following him or not. I made a long face and kept walking.

It was noon.

I felt famished. The food I had eaten in the morning was completely digested. We must reach home. It will take some more time. Even if I wanted to ask him to buy me something to eat, how would that be possible now?

Am I not angry with him?

I did not say anything.

We waited for the bus that went to Sinthamanipudur. More people came in two to three horse-drawn carriages and mingled with the waiting crowd. Thus, a larger crowd was formed.

The people who knew each other continued to talk.

The strangers stared impatiently into the distance.

Some sat down in the shade.

I, too, waited, melting in the midday heat, thinking that my pride was more important than hunger.

When the horn sounded, all eyes turned in its direction.

The people sitting on the ground straightened up. They grabbed their luggage and waited anxiously.

A dark green bus came and stopped near the crowd, its horn sounding.

Although there was a small scuffle to get on the bus, we both got on first. In the commotion, I had deliberately forgotten that I was holding onto my father's arm. We were sitting right behind the driver.

Once again, as I sat close to him, I felt nauseous.

It was such a disgusting sight. I decided that I would never ride with him to the Gounder homes again. What was he doing there?

I remembered.

The room stank as he cleaned and bandaged the old women's legs, and pus oozed out. It stank more of the smell of their mouths when they smiled with their toothless gums. I thought the smell was still lingering in my nostrils.

I wanted to throw up.

Without his knowledge, I smelled my father sitting next to me.

Oh, the same smell. I held my nose and moved away. I moved so far away that my body didn't touch him.

He understood. With a sly smile, he looked at me from the side.

"Get in the bus quickly. Get in… "

I was stunned to hear the roar right in front of me. It was the bus driver turning around, shifting his body, trying to force the passengers to move forward. Startled, I looked at him. His face frightened me even more.

Dark and bloated in the face. A thick moustache. His figure and voice frightened me. I moved closer to my father. I decided it was better to endure the stench than to scream in fear.

I directed my gaze to the ground, not daring to look at him again. At this point, I was attracted by his thick moustache. I raised my eyes because I wanted to see him again.

My gaze fell into his eyes. Our eyes met. His dark face brightened. He twisted his mouth and smiled, showing off his beedi-tinted teeth. Although I averted my eyes, almost startled, I returned his smile.

He began to steer the vehicle, which was teeming with people. The bus drove down the long, dark road.

Even the hot wind blowing into the bus could not keep me from sleeping. Hungry and tired, my eyes half closed, I leaned against my father's shoulders. He held me close. With a smile, he teased me as I snuggled close to him.

"Why, Uma? Do not I stink?"

"Yes, you do stink. But I am tired."

He laughed and hugged me tightly. I was getting angry.

"Do not laugh. Didn't you think it was gross to touch them? Pus was oozing out of one grandmother's leg. The smell was disgusting!"

I frowned.

Not only my words but also my face reflected my dislike for them. Suddenly my father asked me.

"Uma, what did you call her now?"

"Grandma" I said, looking at him and wondering why he was asking that.

"So, you know she's a grandmother, Uma?" he asked, putting his hand on my shoulders.

"If she was your grandmother, would not I have done the same thing, Uma? Wouldn't you? If your grandmother had pain in her arms or feet, wouldn't you massage her?"

"Of course, I would. If she's my grandmother, I'd do anything."

He took my immediate response seriously. "Ah, yes. You would if she was your grandmother. But these oldies are not your grandmothers, are they?" He continued to look deep into my eyes.

"You know why you are not able to see her as your grandmother? Because you are small. Your mind is also small. When Uma and Uma's mind grow up, you will understand."

"And when will I grow up?" Hearing my innocent question, my father teased me.

"There's still time. First you have to grow tall."

My father teased me for being small. This went through my mind as I asked him my next question.

"You are not tall either. Then how did you grow up? How did your mind grow?"

Suddenly, the bus came to a stop with a loud roar. The burning smell of rubber spread all over the place. Those who were sleeping, standing or sitting woke up and became aware of their surroundings again. People said many things without knowing what had happened. Some blamed the driver.

The dog is also a living being. He has a life. How can I kill him? So, I braked hard."

The driver justified himself.

"What you said is right. You stopped to avoid hitting the dog. But we hit our faces on the railing. We are hurt."

Said the old man sitting behind us, a little annoyed. The driver turned around and smiled. The passenger tilted his head and frowned at the smile.

The black dog that had jumped across the road hid under a palm frond, oblivious to the confusion it was causing.

My father smiled at me, who sat in panic. I repeated my question.

"How could you do these things when you are so small?"

"These ..." he said, combing my hair with his fingers.

"I learned about these things late. Otherwise, I would have grown tall, too."

I must be growing up. I made a mental note of it. Silently, I looked outside and saw the trees running behind us.

The villagers called my father Compounder Balan. He was not a compounder. Balakrishnan, who was born and brought up in Kadampuzha, Palakkad, turned into Compounder Balan when he reached Sinthamanipudur in Coimbatore. His childhood dream was to become a doctor. Falling prey to the unyielding habits of his uncle who managed the affairs of his matrilineal family, he had run away. He reached Coimbatore after wandering in many places. It was the early sixties. At that time, there were few basic facilities like hospitals. When people got sick, they went to local healers. They tried the herbal medicines prescribed. In Coimbatore, my father happened to come across Dr. Punyavanam. He was the only MBBS doctor there. There was no hospital. The doctor visited the patients in their homes. He started assisting the doctor and gradually he became known as "Compounder".

When Punyavanam Doctor visits patients, my father goes there periodically to give them injections and medicines. He kept the medicines and injections in an orange chest. The chest and Compounder Balan were a relief to the villagers.

Until his marriage, my father worked as an assistant to the doctor. After his marriage, he took a job at the mill in Sinthamanipudur and started living there. Whenever his time permitted, he went around with his suitcase. Many sick people were waiting for him there.

Once we were on our way back from a similar trip. Since it was a Saturday, a holiday for the mill, he set out with the medicine case, and when I begged him, he took me with him. But I never thought it would be such an unbearable journey.

We went to the Gounders Colony. In those days Gounders were comparatively better off. The brick houses were big. Their courtyards were large. Many people lived in one house. Small and large, people of different ages.

The person who needed my father's care lived in a makeshift shed near the house. I followed him and went inside as well. The large yard and tiled house are only a facade. The sight inside the shed was pitiful. When we entered, the foul smell of a human body hit our noses.

We saw an old woman moaning on a cot in a dark corner of the room. At times she screamed in pain. When she saw my father, her cries grew louder.

"Oh, brother... Compounder, this pain is fatal... Please bandage my wound."

There are so many who struggle like this, past their best days. As they age, they struggle because of various illnesses, wounds and severe pain. In the end, they are thrown to the sidelines of life. Without anyone to take care of them, they end up in such sheds. These are the moments when we realize the triviality of human life.

While letting go of my hand, my father went to her. He sat down next to her on her cot. He lifted the shabby cloth from her knee. What I saw disgusted me. Pus oozed from the wounds on both legs. The room, with hardly any light or ventilation, was filled with an unbearable stench. I did not move from where I was standing.

The old woman was screaming in pain again.

"If you have any medicine to relieve my pain, please give it to me.... Or kill me now... I can't take it anymore." Unable to see her pain, Achen (Father) stroked her with his hand, over her hair.

"Please, don't talk like that." Achen opened the trunk. Took out the orange gloves and put them on. He took some water in a bucket, sat huddled next to her on the floor and cleaned her legs. I stood there covering my eyes. The repulsive smell that entered my nostrils filled my mind with images I did not want to see. When I took a look after some time, he had already covered the wounds with medicine. Her face brightened as her pain subsided.

My father patted her hand and tried to comfort her. "You don't have to be afraid. I will give you pain tablets now."

She smiled in her relief. She waved her hand at me, who was standing near the door. When she saw me, her eyes brightened, she was relieved of her pain.

"Come to me, little one. You look so cute. What's your name?"

Achen nodded in agreement, while I reluctantly moved close to her. I moved forward a little. Keeping some distance so she would not touch me, I said

"Uma."

Her eyes grew wide. She looked at me kindly.

"Oh, that's the name of the goddess Uma, a good name."

Achen pulled me close to her. With her wrinkled hand she pinched my cheek affectionately. Suddenly, I turned my head. I backed away and checked to see if she had a wound on her hand.

I confirmed that her hands looked fine. That made me feel better right away. All I wanted to do was run away from this place of stench.

My father did none of this for money. Nevertheless, in their joy, the Gounders packed gifts like rice or ragi for him. They needed the help of Compounder Balan. He never took any of them home. He always gave them away to the colonies of the Chakliars, who do manual scavenging. Although there were only three or four families living there, their families were large. The men worked as scavengers. Their wives worked in the nearby cast iron factory. They were paid a small wage for filling iron into baskets with the help of magnets. They even had their nursing babies bundled on their backs while they worked.

That day also, we walked from Gounders Colony to Chakliars Colony, and when we got there a horde of children swarmed around us like crows. They were not dressed properly. Most of the children crowded around us had dirt and mud on their bodies, and their noses were running, too. My father lifted one of them on his shoulder. Others started laughing loudly. "Hold him down." He helped him blow his nose with his right hand. I lost control when I saw Achen cleaning him with his right hand. I stood there all upset. Every day Achen fed me a bite of rice mixed with curd. At that moment, I decided not to take that morsel out of his hand. I wanted to throw up. We were sitting on the porch of a house.

"Eat, dear, eat. It's freshly prepared."

Some kozhukkattai (sweet rice dumplings) were brought in a leaf.

Although I was hungry and my heart was heavy at what I saw there, I did not even feel like looking at it. The lady's shabby dress and the gloomy ambience disgusted me. He took a kozhukkattai from the leaf and ate it. Since he read my thoughts by my uneasiness, he did not force me to eat it.

While my father was eating it, I looked at him in disgust.

I sensed that it was not my father. I saw an ugly creature with ruptured abscesses and purulent mucus. Full of fear, I turned my head away. For a moment I closed my eyes tightly.

When I opened my eyes, I saw a naughty boy sitting on his lap, trying in vain to eat the candy. His gestures made me laugh. My heart cooled down.

That evening, as I sat at dinner, my father made a rice ball, rolled in curd, and offered it to me. Suddenly, I replayed those scenes in my mind. The old woman with the sores and the children with their runny noses. But beyond those scenes, he reached out to me with the rice ball. Without thinking further about it, I opened my mouth and swallowed it. He smiled at me and asked,

"What is it, Uma?"

I looked him in the eye and expressed my wish.

"Father, I want to grow up to be like you. When will I be?"

With his eyes wide open, he looked at me with love.

"To grow up, you must eat well. Then you will become as tall as me."

From then on, I ate a ball of rice from my father every night and walked to the pillar with the areca palm near the kitchen. On it I marked my height. Every day I checked repeatedly whether I was growing taller or not.

TWO

"What do you want me to do? I do not know anything about math. If the gentleman breaks a leg or an arm and stops coming to school, I would be very happy."

I suppressed a sob as I said this, and Thankamani was sad too.

"Does it hurt too much? Show me." She sat down next to me, who was in pain, and asked.

I lifted my knee-length skirt and showed it to her. On the pale flesh of my thigh, the bruise Subbarayan sir had given me stood out. The sight of that ugly, painful mark made me cry again. I cried. Thankamani comforted me.

"Okay, okay. You don't have to cry. It's going to be all right. "

I yelled at her in a mixture of fear and anger.

"How is it going to be okay? I do not know anything about math. How then? "

"I do not like math. "

"And I do not like the math teacher either. "

Most of the children of the millworkers went to Kathirinmel School. There, everything was free. Even the uniform clothes and the books. Once a year, a few times, on special occasions, you might have to spend a little more money, but otherwise everything is free.

Thankamani and I went to the same class. Thankamani, tall, slim and dark, looked beautiful. She was two years older than me. Because she was 'good' at learning, she came to my class! There were girls and boys in the class. There were also many boys who, like Thankamani, went to the same class for more than a year. Ganeshan and Palanichamy were also part of this group.

Ganeshan refused to give up his studies even though he was taller than most of the teachers. He justified himself by saying that he was not ungrateful enough to leave them.

"Hey, shorty (*kuttachy*)! Every day you get slapped by that cheapskate. Why are you like this?"

Every day Ganeshan teased me about being punished by the math teacher. Hearing it, the others would laugh at me. There were two things he mentioned. First, that I was punished by Mr. Subbarayan. Second, that I was small and always sat in the first seat, on the first bench. It was like that even in the first grade. It did not change even in the eighth grade. Since my fifth-grade year, I have tried to become taller. The column of areca palm next to the work area in the kitchen kept telling me that I had not gotten much taller. But so what? I got the nickname 'shorty.' The other day, as usual, I got beat up by the math teacher and was sad.

"Hey, I will tell you a way to avoid getting beat up by him." Murmured Hemalatha, who comes to school with a double braid of hair and a round bindi, in my ear. Apart from Thankamani, Hemalatha and Mary Lilly, are my closest friends in the class.

I looked at her lovingly, wanting to know my way to save myself. She sat closer to me and said seriously,

"Let me bring you the picture of a god. If you keep it at home and pray, he will not even turn around to look at you."

Hearing Hemalatha talk to me secretly, Thankamani and Mary Lilly became curious. I told them about the solution I had received from Hemalatha. Looking intently into our eyes, she said this and it sounded more believable.

"Whatever you wish for before this God will happen. If you wish for his arm to be broken, it will happen. If it is a leg, yes, it will be. "

The three of us looked at each other. We took Hemalatha into our confidence.

I could not sleep that night thinking of the god who possessed such special powers. I must put an end to the plague of the math teacher. I will pray for him to break his arm. He is tormenting me so much.

It is because I cannot understand math. Is this how I should be punished?

"Uma, come here, where are you? Do this sum on the blackboard."

I felt that the teacher took a certain cruel pleasure in punishing me. Not a day went by when he didn't ask me to do a sum on the blackboard. I never managed to give him the answer he wanted. Nothing good happened except that I lost some nice skin on my thigh. Subbarayan sir was not a frightening figure. Nevertheless, the image of a demon came to my mind whenever I thought of him.

The next day, I went to school exuberantly. I still believed that the image Hemalatha had brought would magically help me pass all the math exams of my life. On the way to school, Thankamani kept asking me many things. I answered nonchalantly with a nod, yes or no.

We arrived earlier than usual. We ran into the classroom and

looked for Hemalatha. She was not there yet. I waited anxiously for her at the classroom door.

"What's the matter, shorty? What are you looking at outside the door?" Ganeshan started mocking me.

I ignored his taunts, pursed my lips, and continued to wait at the door.

When I saw her coming from afar, I felt an indefinable ecstasy, which I had never experienced in my life. I thought Hemalatha looked even prettier that day. Without wasting any time, I ran to her.

She came toward me, a bit more pompous, as if she would be the cause of a great change in my life. But I ignored it. She held my hand and sat down on the bench. When she made sure no one was watching, she opened her light blue bag, took out a book with a brown paper cover, and took a picture. She held it out to me and said,

"Here it is. Keep it safe. Don't tell anyone, don't show anyone."

I looked at it with respect. A radiant figure. A face that exuded kindness. Hemalatha sat close to me and described the picture.

"This is the image of Lord Ayyappa, who is very powerful. It is very difficult to get there. The path goes along the hills, uneven with stones and thorny bushes. Every year my parents go there and walk all the way. "

When she said this with much piety, I could not take my eyes off her. I was ready to take on any road, no matter how rocky, to pave my difficult path in math. I began to feel love for Hemalatha.

I had only one picture of Swami Vivekananda at my home. Since there was no regular pooja or prayers at my home, I did not pay attention to Lord Ayyappa. No one spoke to me about the greatness of Lord Ayyappa. When I reached home, I placed the picture of Lord Ayyappa next to the picture of Vivekananda, closed my eyes for a moment and prayed.

The next day I reached the school with high hopes.

But Subbarayan sir destroyed them.

"Stretch out your hands. You are not learning, but disturbing those who are also learning. Why do you talk to them unnecessarily?"

"Tup " the blow of the slender cane painfully jolted my whole body from the palm. My fingers went numb. I looked at them to see if they were broken. Because my eyes were getting moist, my vision was also fading.

"If you don't sit still, I am going to hit you some more."

His anger did not subside. I thought my misery in math would end with prayer. I was punished twice. As usual, he punished me generously for my math mistakes. I also got a sound caning for blabbing in class.

Wincing in pain, I stared at Hemalatha as if to scorch her. With a helpless expression on her face, she looked down at the ground.

After that incident, I began to hate Hemalatha every time I saw her, with her double-plaited hair and her round bindi.

While I was depressed about the futility of prayer, Mary Lilly came like an angel and told me about an idea she had. She spoke eloquently about the unfailing fruitfulness of prayer. Her words fell like a rain of honey.

She spoke about people who have accomplished things through prayer and gave examples.

When she finished her sermon about people whose illnesses were cured by prayer, about people whose lives were nourished by prayer, I thought she was the angel born to drive the devil called Subbarayan out of my life. I sat there and looked at her. I felt that she had a halo around her.

The gospel of Mary Lilly gave me new strength.

She gave me a small picture of Mother Mary. I put it in the palm of my hand. Mary Lilly said, "The Mother who is in my palm holds the whole world in her hand." Believing that the Mother would help me correct my false sums, I repeated the prayers she taught me.

That night I went to bed rejuvenated.

The day came.

In the math class, Subbarayan sir also came. Everyone stood up and greeted him. I stood up, closed my eyes, and meditated on the mother I held tightly in the palm of my hand. I recited in my heart the prayer Mary Lilly had taught me.

"Mother, may you hear my prayer... May my sums never go

wrong. Let me escape punishments, O Mother, who art the guardian of all life, protect me."

In my zeal for prayer, I did not notice that I was squeezing the Mother in my hand. I did not notice that all the other students had taken their seats after the formal greeting and that Subbarayan sir was staring at me.

I was at the zenith of my prayers. I opened my eyes when I heard the teacher shouting.

"Why are you sleeping so early in the morning? What kind of impudence is this?"

Subbarayan sir was trembling with anger. The whole class shook and laughed. My hands and legs were shaking. The mother herself, feeling safe in the palm of my hand, giggled, I thought.

The usual routine did not change.

I had enough of Subbarayan sir. The pain, the sorrow, the shame. I did not talk to anyone. Thankamani tried to comfort me. I did not say anything to her either.

At lunch time, I took the figure of Mother and hid it in the toilet. I was afraid that I would get more punishment if I kept it with me. I came back and sat down in class without talking to anyone.

"How arrogant you are to keep the picture of Our Lady in the toilet!"

I heard a sound as if I had been slapped in the face, turned around and saw Mary Lilly glaring angrily at me.

"Isn't that enough for you? You deserve more."

She showered me with profanity. I looked at her and could

not understand what was going on. I wanted to ask her, " Your bad advice got me into trouble, and now you want to devour me? But her attitude made me wary, and I decided to keep quiet.

She would not let me finish.

"You are insolent, haughty and arrogant. Nothing can change you."

I looked at her again and found in her hand the figurine of Mother Mary that I had left in the toilet. That made her lose her temper. I was disobeying her God. She believed that I had denigrated Mother Mary.

I kept repeating my mistakes in maths. When I had resolved never to pray for sums again so that I would not make mistakes, Thankamani brought a new plan into play.

She asked me to try that too. She enticed me with a picture she had torn off a piece of paper. Lord Shiva in tandava pose. The Lord was glowing with fiery anger.

I prayed only once.

Since my two previous prayers to escape Subbarayan sir's punishment had failed, I prayed less fervently this time.

But the prayer was soon fulfilled.

While boarding a bus, sir slipped and fell, injuring his right arm. As soon as she heard about this incident,

Thankamani got scared. She feared that someone would come to know that my prayer was the reason for this mishap. Although I had said the prayer, she became impatient that her involvement in the conspiracy would soon be revealed.

I comforted her and told her that no one would know. But Mary Lilly was determined not to let her chance slip away. She was waiting to take revenge on me for disrespecting her God. She pranced around with joy. She was going to seize the opportunity that came her way.

"I know that you have said some prayers. That is why sir's arm is broken. I will not fail to tell him. I will go now and tell him to wait."

She became a lion and I became a deer. Thankamani became as small as a rabbit. She was so angry that she wanted to tear us to pieces and eat us. She kept repeating that Mother Mary herself had given her this opportunity.

"You kept Mother Mary in the washroom, didn't you? This is the reason... For Mother's sake, this is the retribution I am giving you."

I wanted to find a way to persuade Mary. To seduce her.

It was the only way.

I thought I would seduce her with something she liked.

I sat down close to her. "Do not, do not talk to me." She turned her face away and looked angry with me. I touched her pleadingly on the shoulder.

"Let me buy you some dry dates from the aunty who sits outside the school gate. Salted or spicy, whichever you like."

She seemed to have taken that well. She gave me a look. I repeated.

"Do not, my dear. Do not say anything… I will buy what you like."

Thankamani, who knew she liked dry dates and gooseberries, coaxed her too.

"Yes, my dear. She will buy you, if she says so, don't say anything about her."

Mary Lilly did not say whether she had given in or not. Her indifference annoyed us even more.

When the maths lesson came, my hands and legs started shaking. Everyone greeted Subbarayan sir as he entered the class, his arm hanging from a white string around his neck. This included the trembling voices of both Thankamani and me.

He sat down on the chair after looking at everyone. I looked at him to see what was coming now. My gaze met his eyes. Without hesitation, he called me over, shaking my head.

"Uma, come here."

My heart trembled. I knew I was trapped. But how did he know? I thought so too. I glanced sharply at Mary Lilly. Had she told him before class?

She looked at me pityingly, as if she knew nothing.

I gritted my teeth.

Thankamani sat there with her eyes closed. As if she did not want to see even if the sky had fallen.

Like a convict ready to accept any punishment, I walked towards sir. He eyed me from head to toe and then said to the class.

"There are no assignments to solve today. You will all sit quiet".

While I stood there wide-eyed, he continued.

"If anyone in the class makes noise, write down their names and give them to me. Make sure the class does not make any noise."

I stood in that exact spot and could not believe it. It took me a moment to regain my composure. I looked first at Thankamani.

She was sitting there with her mouth wide open. Unable to understand what was going on. For the first time I felt sympathy for Subbarayan sir. It was the first time he addressed me with love. This incident shocked Mary Lilly the most. She stared at the ground till the end of that class.

It was not the gods who helped me correct my mistakes in maths but Ganeshan who had failed many classes and joined me as a classmate.

"You, shorty, you are not mad at maths, you are mad at the maths teacher."

One day, like a psychologist, he explained my problem to me.

"Do you know why...? He pinches your thigh. That's the problem... Go and tell him... Don't pinch me... You can hit me with the ruler."

I felt that Ganeshan was right. I, who could study well in all other subjects, couldn't cope with maths because I was afraid of the teacher who taught it. I went to Subbarayan sir and spoke to him as Ganeshan had said. It sounded like a threat. There was no one else in the staff room.

"Sir. Don't pinch me anymore. If I make a mistake, slap my hand." He glared at me. I said it in a serious tone.

"Otherwise, I'll report it to the headmaster."

It worked. From then on, Subbarayan sir never pinched me again. I felt respect for Ganeshan who advised me to respond. I also brought home the gods of Hemalatha, Thankamani and Mary Lilly.

When my father noticed my unusual behaviour, he asked me the reason.

"Lack of god is the cause of all problems."

My father laughed and said, "We cannot accommodate all the gods of the world in our house. Uma, let them be where they're. Always remember. All the gods are the same. They just have different names."

I stared at him, for I didn't understand what he was saying.

"Yes, the gods don't quarrel among themselves. We, the humans, argue in the name of the gods."

As he spoke, I was busy keeping each god in its proper place.

THREE

In the royal court of the Chola king Kanikannan, Uraiyoor Manivannan is held captive. He raises his voice against the king who is preparing to punish him. MGR plays Manivannan.

There is unending applause for each of his dialogues. I could not watch MGR being punished, with his arms tied behind his back, a long pole between them and a chain around his neck. I could not bear to see him tied up.

The film *Mannadimannan* was shown in a theatre called Lakshmi tent kottai. This was the only place in the village where films were shown. The same film could run there for three years at a stretch.

At the age of five, I started getting addicted to cinema. MGR was the hero of my heart. Every day I would go to the cinema just to see MGR. Lakshmi tent kottai was not far from my house. It was a shed covered with palm fronds. We watched a film while sitting on the muddy floor. It only cost fifty paisa. To sit on a bench in the back cost one rupee. Even if I had a rupee, I would never like to watch a film on a bench. It's not like sitting on the floor is particularly comfortable. If I sit close to the screen, I can see MGR up close. I would only take tickets for the first two or three days. Later, I would go in without fear to see it without a ticket, as if I belonged there. The person who tore the ticket at the door did not mind either. Sometimes Thankamani kept my company. Her mother kept a tight rein on her. "Girls should not go to the cinema alone. Modesty and submission are the adornment of girls. Girls without them are defiant." Thankamani's mother was wise enough to write a good essay describing the virtues of a girl of good character. Thus, modesty and a sense of submission that was far ahead of her age grew up in Thankamani.

"More...hit him more..." I once shouted as I watched MGR beat his opponents. Sitting on the ground, I threw up the mud in my excitement.

"Hey, Uma, what is this? Why are you throwing the sand around? See, it falls on everyone."

Thankamani held my hand vigorously and reprimanded me as I flung the mud around. I did not listen to her scolding. My admiration for MGR grew stronger even though many tried to reprimand me for it. I never stopped throwing dust when he threw his enemies to the ground.

"Naan aanaiyittal, athu nadanthu vitttai, intha ezhaikal vedanai padamaattaar, uyirullavare oru thunbamillai, avar kanneerkkadalile vizhamattaar.

If I order it, if it happens, the unfortunate one will not suffer; as long as there is life, we will not suffer; he will not fall into a sea of tears."

I wrote this song in my notebook and memorized it. I sang this song MGR wearing white trousers and a black shirt and holding a whip.

"Uma, this song was sung by T. M. Sounder Rajan sir, not by MGR. It is just that he has featured in this song."

My father tried to correct me because he knew how much I liked MGR. But I claimed he did not know anything about it.

" No, it's just MGR who sang the song."

Then it's my turn to sing and dance to the song. I use my father's bath towel instead of the whip.

I twirl it towards him and pretend MGR did it. Hearing me, he would run for his life.

There is a cemetery on the way from my house to the theatre. The road bends just after it. Women used to avoid passing this area at night. But I used to take this street when

I went to the cinema. People knew that I took this street to watch films even if I was alone. Since my father had no problem with it, no one had a problem with it. Thankamani's mother always tried to convince my father.

"What is it? She is young, a little girl. Why do you let her go to the cinema all by herself?"

My father would cut her short, knowing that her description follows a virtuous woman.

"No trouble, elder sister; she is only in our familiar neighbourhood; why are you worried?"

She did not like that at all. "Oh, you will not understand now; you have spoilt your girl by pampering her too much."

Though she knew her advice would fall on deaf ears, she kept repeating it to my father.

That evening too, I watched the film *Padagotti* alone, starring MGR, Saroja Devi and MN Nambiar. It was my third time. The story is about a fight between two gangs. MGR plays the icon of goodness and mercy. I walked past the graveyard and sang the song MGR sings for the character played by Saroja Devi.

"*Thotral poo malarum/ thodaamale naan malarnthen/ Suttal pon sivakkum, sudaamal kan sivanthen,*

"Touch it and the flower will bloom.
Untouched, I have blossomed.
Ignite it, and the gold will turn red.
My eyes are red without fire."

"*Thotral poo malarum*

Touch it, and the flower will blossom"

I was startled by the sudden shouts.
Not one person, but a whole crowd. I stopped singing.

Without knowing it, my song stopped.

My throat went dry. It's the abandoned graveyard.

What more does it take to get scared? My body went numb, from the tip of my toes to the crown of my head. I heard the scream again as I began to run with my eyes closed. It too came from the same bend. But this time it was only one. I heard loud laughter as I turned to run in the opposite direction and looked over. Then I could breathe again.

"What's that? Very frightened? Did you see a ghost? We only did that to scare you... "

It was a prank by the older boys in the area. But such things did not end my association with Lakshmi Kottai. On the nights I went to the movies alone, MGR became my hero.

I bought the books with the lyrics of the films and sang to my heart's content. Every dialogue of MGR was imprinted in my mind as a principle. The views of MGR have influenced the character building of the Tamil people. Whether in cinema or in real life, most of the films he acted in were meant to steer society in the right direction. All the characters he played stood up for justice.

They stood up for truth and justice. They conveyed the ultimate victory of these virtues. Even in the songs he performed, the lyrics give the message to walk uprightly in life.

"*Thirudaathe pappa thirudaathe*"

Do not steal, child... Do not do it"
This is an advice to the children to be honest.

"*Thirudanaay pathu thirunthaa vittal thiruttai ozhikka mudiyath*"

If you see a thief and do not correct him, you cannot eradicate theft....

It teaches the importance of correcting wrong behaviour.

" *Thoonkaathe, thambi thoonkaathe.*"

It reminds children that if they sleep now, they will not be able to sleep later.

When I was in grade six, MGR visited Kathirinmel School. I was the one who gave him a rose to welcome him to the school anniversary. When I handed him the flower, I touched his fingers. He kissed me on the cheek. Touching my hero! Getting a little kiss from him. How lucky I was!

In my childhood I spoke fluent Tamil, and that had its advantages. When elections were announced, I was invited to make public announcements. For whom do I canvass for votes? For MGR himself.

"*Peranpudeya periyorkale/ thaymarkale/unkaluku ponnana vaakkukake/irattayila chihnathilvvaakkalithu/ puratchi thalaivan MGR avarkale vetri varumcheyyumaru/unkal vote irattayilaykku/podungAmma vote/irattaiyilaye paathu.*"

Dear elders and mothers, cast your precious votes on the Twin Leaf symbol and let the revolutionary leader Dr. MGR win. Your votes for Twin Leaf. Cast your vote for Twin Leaf.

In every corner of my village, at every crossroads, my voice echoed.

"Isn't that Uma, Compounder Balan's child?" People were talking as they saw me sitting in a jeep, microphone in hand, canvassing for votes.

When I saw them watching me, I became excited and announced,

"Cast your vote. With the symbol of Twin Leaf. "

They would pay me five rupees for announcing from morning till night. My eyes were not on the money but on canvassing for votes for MGR. Not only in his films, but also in real life, he maintained his compassion for the poor.

He proved the value of truth, righteousness and justice. I have never cried so much as when MGR died. I cried all day and caught a fever.

Thousands of people flock to the grave of MGR in Marina. Some bow down before him and talk to him about their sorrows. Others hold their ears close to the grave. From there they hear a sound: tick, tick. Some believe that he is still trying to tell them something. Some say that his watch, which he was wearing when he was buried, still works.

Among the elderly, there are some who still do not believe that MGR has died. Although I have come to terms with the fact that he is no longer alive, I sometimes feel that he

is telling me his dialogues in person.

One has a certain responsibility towards the society in which one lives. If you forget about them and only care about yourself, neither we nor our country will prosper.

Did not MGR tell me that himself when he kissed me on the cheek while I held a rose petal in my right hand, wide-eyed and amazed?

FOUR

Our house in Sinthamanipudur was hardly a kilometre away from Irugur railway station. From our house we could hear the whistle of the train. Especially at night. Our house in Sinthamanipudur belonged to Thankamani's family. We lived there on rent. This village was mainly inhabited by factory workers and their families. There were houses in a row. All of them had walls made of mud. The floor was plastered with cow dung. They all had only basic amenities. Every morning, people painted *kolams* in front of the house with rice flour.

When I was five years old, I learnt how to paint *kolams*. Amma (mother) taught me. She amazed me with her skill. She had very dexterous fingers. Though I am not that good, I too learnt how to clean up and paint *kolam* in the morning.

My father motivated me. When he came home after his night duty, he would wait quietly behind me and watch me draw. Sometimes he would sit beside me on the floor and help me by handing me the rice flour. Without hiding his joy, he called out to Amma as he entered the house, "Look at the *kolam* Uma made. It looks nothing like what a small child has painted!" I pricked up my ears eagerly to hear Amma's reply. But she never said a good word about it.

She did not mind cleaning the yard and painting *kolams*. But she was more interested in applying kohl on her eyes beforehand. She was very particular about maintaining her appearance. My mother was a fair, slim and pretty woman. Her house was in Pazhayannoor. Thankamani of the Nambalatt house came to Sinthamanipudur as

Balakrishnan, my father made her his wife. When they got married, he was not yet a worker in the mill.

He was simply the compounder Balan who assisted Doctor Punyavanam. His job of carrying the doctor's bag like a servant was beneath her. She did not like it when the villagers affectionately called him Compounder.

The stories say that their quarrels over this increased during the first years of marriage and he was forced to accept work at the mill.

Only what happened after the age of five has stuck in my memory. The rest are the stories I heard. But my later life proves that what I heard was not just made up.

Although he took the job at the mill, he did not completely stop working as a compounder. On holidays, he would travel with his suitcase. Many people waited for him in the houses of the Gounder and Chakliar colonies. Amma gave us a 'grand' welcome when we returned from such trips.

"The father and daughter are back, having wandered about in all sorts of places. They are already lost. Why don't you leave her alone and stop spoiling her?"

Amma used me in her war against Achen. He kept quiet most of the time. That was how conflicts were avoided.

There were many fights over the women in the Chakliars colony. They did not lack children, although they did not have enough to eat or clothes. No one cared to check the births. After seeing their pathetic conditions in person, he forced them to look into family planning. Using his ESI card, he took them to the hospital and forced them to use family planning methods. According to the hospital records, the cleaner women of Chakliars Colony thus became wives of Balakrishnan.

"Who is she? Are not you ashamed to present this slovenly animal as your wife?"

Amma had somehow come to know about these things. She went into a frenzied state as if she was possessed by the goddess Kali. Sometimes Achen too would go into fits of rage. He would lose control and fly into a rage. He will attack her and complain that she is crossing the line by adorning herself too much. He will rebuke her and say that as the wife of a mill worker, she should not crave the life of the mill owner's wife. His reasoning was not entirely pointless.

She bought a lot of sarees with different patterns. She polished her hair with Keshavardhini oil. It had a pungent smell. When she went out, she only put on Vicco turmeric cream, face powder and lipstick. My father asked her why she should dress up like that to go to clothes shops or markets When she heard that, she repeated the same reason.

"You should learn how to live a good life. There is no point in wiping the noses of the cleaners' children or wiping the boils of the Gounder's wives."

Then my father would fall silent. She knows there is no other stronger weapon to shut my father up.

There were some rules Amma had imposed on my father when he returned from his routine visits to the Gounders' houses. He was not to enter the house without washing his hands, feet and face with soap. He was not to bring anything they gave him to take home. Not even rice, ragi or sweets. He followed these commandments scrupulously, like a good samaritan. His justification would help improve world peace.

He believed in the adage that it takes two to tango. But it was not always adhered to. Most of the time they quarrelled. Their quarrels did not stay within the four walls of our house. When I played with Thankamani and other friends on the street, Thankamani's mother would goad me about their quarrels. Since I was engrossed in my game, they did not hear much from me.

The arrival of the storytelling group called *'Annanmar Kadhakal'* marks one of the festive seasons in Sinthamanipudur. Once a year they come to our village. Their performers, wearing different costumes, recite four to five stories. The performances take place in the evening. People come after work and watch the programme. The group consisted of four people. One plays a female role. One drums. Two sing and tell the stories. The people in this village provided their food and shelter. In our village, food was organized every day in a local house. Amma's great cooking skills came out when it was our turn to serve the food to the troupe. Amma had prepared more dishes for them than in ordinary homes.

Amma grew closer to the storytelling troupe. For them, there was nothing more than a preference for a house where good food was served. By giving them milk, eggs and other things, Amma created a good rapport with them. *Nallavan Vazhka* and *Chilappathikaram* were the two main stories they told. There was a handsome man in the troupe who played the female roles. He looked so handsome in female attire that the women became envious of his looks. When they finished playing a story, the audience paid money and that was their main source of income. At the end of a month, they had a considerable sum together. When the *Annanmaar Sangham* confirmed that they would be back soon with new stories and thanked them for the food and accommodation, we children were sad to say goodbye to them. But as soon as they left, the loud arguments at my house increased so much that I forgot all about it.

My father's voice became louder than usual. Amma's lack of responsiveness was even stranger. She maintained an unusual silence. He went into fits of rage. His expression changed when Thankamani's mother whispered something to him on the way: Thankamani's mother was talking about the man who plays female roles in *Annanmar Sangham*. He was on his way home from work. Thankamani's mother was waiting for him on the veranda of the house. She came out on the road as soon as she saw my father. As my father approached, she looked around and murmured,

"You see, you must listen to me patiently. The guy who plays the female roles in *Annanmar Sangham* told me this when they left …"

Hearing the whisper, he was unusually panicked. What would the guy playing female roles say? He looked at her in wonder. After making sure no one was near her, she continued.

"Do you know what he said? I am married and have three children. This is the only source of income for me.

If I get into trouble here too, it will be a problem for me and my family."

My father stood there as if he did not understand anything. Thankamani's mother spoke bluntly. It seemed Amma wanted to go with the guy who played women's roles. Hearing this, he got scared and begged Thankamani's mother. He begged her not to harm him.

He adjusted the shoulder strap of his bag and went home in silence. Thankamani's mother spoke a little louder.

"Balaa... This is something you should know. You need to know about it. So, I told you. Don't say afterwards that you didn't know."

My father, who came into the house like a calm ocean, quickly transformed. His sense of humiliation, anger and pain burst forth.

"Is this what you had in mind when you prepared a sumptuous meal for them, including milk and eggs?"

Even after hearing all this, she remained unmoved. Achen continued to babble. He belched out all his anger in words. Amma surprised us by not speaking a single word.

Their estranged marriage was stormy and turbulent. By now, I had a younger brother. With his birth, Amma's tantrums also increased. When he was six months old, she constantly nagged my father that she could not stay at home and take care of two children. She forced him to look for work for her. He had no choice but to obey her. She got a job as a typist with an Anglo-Indian company called Prema Cottage Industries. It became my duty to look after Thambikuttan when I came home from school. So, my evening games came to a halt.

Once she started working, it became very difficult to see her at all. She would go to work in the morning and come back very late in the evening. She did not care about her children and what they were doing. On Saturdays, she only worked until noon. After that she goes to parties with her Anglo-Indian friends.

On this day, she rushed to the birthday party at the house of Flora, who works with her. My father sensed for the first time that her negligence in housekeeping and childcare was getting out of hand and tried to rebuke her.

"Thankamani, you work as you like. You spend your money as you like. I have no objection to that. Are you worried about this family?"

Amma stood there as if she was not worried even if the sky was falling. She ignored his talk, stood in front of the mirror and brushed her hair. As he lost control, his voice, directed at her image in the mirror, deepened.

"You are disobeying me. At least be considerate of the people around us. At least be aware that this is a village."

She threw the comb against the mirror and shouted.

"I am not afraid of anyone. I will live as I wish. Find someone else to cling to the children."

She was trembling. She screamed hysterically. She threw away everything on the table. Thambikuttan, who was lying on the straw mat in the corner of the room, started crying. I ran to him. I handed him a toy that was lying next to him. In his anger, he threw it away. Suddenly I was startled when I heard the mirror shatter. One of the splinters also fell next to me. I lay down and covered my frightened younger brother, who was crying, so that it would not fall on him. Amma smashed the mirror by throwing a handy brass vessel at it. She could not control her rage and smashed and destroyed everything. Achen tried to hold her by force, but she ran screaming out of the house. She ran to the well, but he dragged her back into the room with all his strength. With a grunt, she sat down on the floor. He held her hands together, ignoring the cruel look on her face, and sat down beside her at the well.

She exhibited symptoms of dementia or epilepsy.

It proved to be a blessing for her. After that, my father did not try to stop her.

As she became more independent, her life became busier with more parties and work. Sometimes Amma would take me to the parties. Once it was a party after an engagement. I was amazed when my mother took me to the party hall. There was no smell of the people or the soil of Sinthamanipudur there. A smell that tempts one to inhale it incessantly. The ladies wore knee-length frocks. The men wore formal suits and coats. Most people filled glasses with frothy, intoxicating drinks. The scene was different, with songs and dances. These previously unknown and unfamiliar sights did not excite me. I just wanted to get away from those bright lights into the yellow sunlight of Sinthamanipudur.

My home resembled a dreary sea where peace reigned only for a short time. Their relationship was deteriorating day by day. Even if they said nothing, they were inwardly preparing for war. Though exhausted by Amma's stubbornness, my father believed that things would get better. In those days, a new person moved into a rented house two houses away. Ponnuchamy was from Tiruchirappalli. Ponnuchamy was well-built, tall and good-looking, though he had a dark complexion. He came to Sinthamanipudur in search of work. The person who had promised him a job in the mill washed his hands off the matter. He tried his luck by waiting in the rented house. His gentle demeanour and friendly attitude helped him. He became more acceptable than even those who had lived there for a long time. As he became familiar and close to the people around him, he had no shortage of food. Soon he also got a job in the mill. With this, Ponnuchamy also became a part of Sinthamanipudur. He also used to get food from our home. Amma packed his food in the stacked lunch box for him. It was my job to bring it to him. I enjoyed that because he had a lot of cinema song books. I'd stay there until he finishes lunch. He will ask about our home. I will be engrossed in the song books and try to memorise at least two lines.

Kovilpatti is two buses away from Sinthamanipudur. That day I went there to attend the birthday party of Stella, Amma's colleague's daughter.

We went there in the afternoon. In the evening, after the party, she bought some sarees from a textile shop in Kovilpatti. The way she acted, I suspected that Amma was a regular customer there. Sarees with different patterns. When we came out of the shop, it was already dark. It is impossible to return to our village the same night. That night we stayed in a house in Kovilpatti. It was quite big. I do not know whose house it was and why we stayed there. As I was very tired from the journey, I fell asleep very quickly. I woke up startled because I felt something crawling up my body. When I opened my eyes, a man was smiling broadly at me. I recognized that it was the man I had met in the textile shop the night before. Judging by his behaviour, I had guessed that he was the owner of the shop. Startled, I looked at him. He was wearing only a dhoti. He was sitting close to me, his hand pressed against my thigh. Screaming, I got up and ran. Amma, who was making tea, heard and came out. He was startled by my screaming.

"Nothing to worry about. Perhaps she was frightened when she saw me... Did you have a bad dream, Uma?" I stood behind Amma as he approached me.

"Oh, that's her usual tantrum when people come near her...

Go, brush your teeth."

Amma did not inquire why I was so upset, or try to assuage my fears, not even with a look. I still felt anxious. Why had I screamed? What was he doing to me? Was it because I saw something and got scared? I actually felt like something was crawling up my body. I actually felt tickled.

No, I did not imagine that; it was not a bad dream.

I kept silent as we boarded the first bus to Sinthamanipudur. People going to the market crowded the bus. The sun was just beginning to get brighter. More and more people appeared at the crossroads. Women selling jasmine flowers; fruit and vegetable vendors by the roadside. The village was slowly waking up. When we boarded the next bus, we sat down next to each other.

"I will tell Achen everything. " I poured out the sorrow in my heart to her. As if she did not understand me, she asked.

"What are you going to tell him?" Anger rose in her eyes. With a sterner tone, she asked me as I sat with my eyes lowered.

"What are you going to tell him?"

"I will tell him ... that he tickled me in my sleep. He scared me in my sleep." I didn't know how to describe it further. Honestly, I did not know what he had done to me. She tried to convince me that it was not a serious matter.

"Nobody has done anything. It's just your feeling. He let us stay with him because he is a good person. You got scared for no reason."

Amma kept repeating that I was imagining it all. But my mind did not come to rest.

When I narrated this incident to my father, I realized that there was an ocean raging inside him that wanted to tear everything down. I understood from the way my father erupted that it was not my feelings. He was in a fit of rage. He lost control and was throwing it left and right.

"I am not good enough to control you. So, you live willfully. Are you going to destroy the life of an innocent child now?"

I too got scared looking at my father with such unusual anger. I hid behind the door. When my father hit her, Amma pushed him away and ran outside. When she heard the noise, Thankamani's mother came out. What happened next was a repeat of what had happened before. She showed symptoms of dementia or epilepsy and rolled on the floor. Thankamani's mother picked her up, brought her into the house and laid her on the bed. After some time, she became calm again.

My father sat on the ground in despair, resting his head

on his arms. Thambikuttan, who is three years old, stood close beside me and held my hand. Achen was completely exhausted. His gestures told me that he was in great turmoil. I felt very guilty. I felt responsible for this scuffle. If I had not said anything, Amma and Achen would not have quarrelled. This situation would not have happened. But quite contrary to my expectations, the dark clouds that were gathering at my house cleared very quickly. The very next day, Amma went to work as if nothing had happened.

This commotion was also short-lived, like the water that accumulates in the narrow streets of Sinthamanipudur after the rain. Just as the water evaporated without a trace from the red earth in the hot sun, everyone forgot about this incident and the commotion it had caused.

Peaceful again. As calm as the sea where the storms had settled.

But it was only a short pause until the next big scene.

This crucial incident occurred the day before Deepavali. In Tamil Nadu, Deepavali is an important festival. It is no different in Sinthamanipudur. We looked forward to setting off firecrackers, lighting lamps and wearing new clothes. My father gets an annual bonus just before Deepavali. As soon as we receive it, we buy clothes to have new clothes sewn. This time was no different.

On Deepavali, me and Thankamani decorate the houses. We also helped decorate the surrounding houses. The walls were painted white with a mixture of lime water and indigo.

On the eve of Deepavali, the women are very busy. The most important task is making the sweets. They make traditional treats like murukku, kuzhalappam and pakka vada.

That day, Amma had also soaked rice and black lentils in our kitchen. I thought she might prepare some sweets. She did not go to work that day. I was not sure if she had taken leave or just did not go. My father was on day duty. He goes in the morning and comes back in the evening.

Until noon, I didn't notice that she had bothered to cook

the sweets. Amma was in a frenzy since my father had left for his work in the morning. I was confused when I saw her packing her clothes into two bags and asked her,

"Are we not making sweets?"

"Yes, of course, Amma will go to Uncle's house and then make the sweets. Let me make the rice and lentil dough there."

I felt happy. How ashamed I would have been if my house had been quiet while all the other houses were busy cooking and roasting!

Amma held out a five rupee note and looked me in the eye as I stood there lost in thought.

"Buy firecrackers; be careful when you burst them." I stretched out my hand to take the money. I thought I was buying sparklers, not firecrackers.

"Then, Uma............" As if remembering something serious, she continued, "Hereafter, you must learn to cook rice and other dishes."

While the sparklers filled my mind, I did not understand the seriousness of her words.

Amma left for the city by bus at 4.20pm. As she left, she took with her the two bags in which she had packed the clothes.

Before it got dark, the people of Sinthamanipudur started lighting the lamps. We heard the noise of firecrackers from different corners. I went and stood in front of the house with Thambikuttan. When my father came home from work that day, he brought a parcel. I ran to him, took the parcel and opened it. Firecrackers. When I saw the different kinds of firecrackers, sparklers and flower pots, I was happy. But where are the clothes for tomorrow?

"They are not ready yet. He still has to sew on the buttons. He said he would bring them over in the morning." Explained my father as I stood there indignantly.

When he entered the house, he was taken aback. There was silence in the kitchen. He went into the kitchen without changing and thought, why is our house so quiet while all the other houses are so busy? There was no one there. He also searched the room.

"Uma, where is Amma?"

I was busy counting the sparklers and the flower pots. Without moving my eyes, I told him,

"She has gone to her uncle's house."

"To the uncle's house? For Deepavali?"

I was still focused on the firecrackers.

My father was panicking. He had a strange feeling. He went into the house and searched again. The soaked rice and lentils were still there. He began to worry. He went into the house and looked in the cupboard. Her clothes were not there. The small radio that was on the table was also gone.

When he came out of the room, he was sweating profusely. In a brittle voice he asked me,

"Uma, when did Amma leave?"

I felt uncomfortable as I sensed the nervousness in his voice.

"Amma left on the 4.20 bus."

I stood up, looked at his face and said that in a moment he seemed as if he had lost all his strength. I too became worried.

"What's wrong, *Acha*? What happened?"

He walked out without saying anything. He called Ranganna, who was working with him. They both rode away on their bicycles.

I stood there stunned. Firecrackers boomed in my ears. Sparklers and flower pots flared up in my eyes.

After some time Thankamani and her mother came and took me and Thambikuttan to their house. We ate the sweets they had made. Together we lit the sparklers and enjoyed it.

I forgot about my father's upset face because of the joy. I forgot the face of my mother who said she would go to her uncle's house and come back. Thankamani, Thambikuttan and I played together and enjoyed ourselves.

The longer the night went on, the more people gathered

around our house. Almost all the people of Sinthamanipudur had come. Not understanding anything, I asked Thankamani's mother about it.

Though she hesitated at first, after much coaxing, she told me that my mother was missing. My Amma, who had gone to her uncle's house, does not seem to have arrived there. My father and Rangannan are still searching. Many others are searching in other directions.

Our house became as silent as a house where death has entered. People crowded in the front yard. They chatted in hushed tones. All the lamps in Sinthamanipudur went out. The noise of firecrackers also died down. Those who went in search of my mother returned disappointed. My father sat leaning against the wall, feeling insulted and holding his head between his knees.

His voice cut through the darkness, the mud wall and the loneliness. Ranganna called out, "Palanichamy has also disappeared."

Suddenly there was a crash in the sky. People saw themselves in the flashes. I wanted to ask my father, who was sitting there with his head hanging and ashamed, if I would get the new dress with the buttons fixed tomorrow.

The petals of the night flower had fully unfurled.

FIVE

As a child, one cannot realize the full seriousness of the reality of life. I did not realize that the chances I lost were irretrievable. But I did understand something. Since I was eight years old, I had to take care of my younger brother and give him the love and affection of a mother. That Deepavali day robbed me of my innocent childhood.

My father did not go out of the house for two days after Amma left.

Was it sadness, insult or embarrassment to look at the faces of the people around him, or the difficulty of leaving us alone? He stayed at home. We survived the first day with the food Thankamani's mother had brought. Achen refused to eat anything. Thankamani's mother scolded him as he lay in bed.

"Balan, your wife has gone away. If you sit like this, who will take care of your children? They still need consideration and care. You get up, eat and go."

Her caring exhortations did not yield any results. The whole day he just lay there. I did not realise at that point that it was such a big problem that she had left. Wasn't it when she was still there?

The next day he got up early in the morning. He tidied the house and cleaned up everything that had fallen into disarray. When I got up, he was busy making idly and sambar. I stood there looking at him, wondering at the change this languishing lover had undergone overnight.

When he noticed me watching him, he asked, "Uma, are you up?"

He looked like a fighter who had gathered enough strength to fight against all odds.

"You have not cleaned the front yard and laid the *kolam* yet. Finish it quickly and come. Wake up Thambikuttan too." He reminded me not to forget my good habits. I was glad he had forgotten his plight. I took a pinch of charcoal flakes from the pot and ran to the well.

For a while it was a struggle between my index finger and my teeth. Then I took the broom and cleaned the front portico. While I was drawing the *kolam*, Thankamani's mother came. Thinking that my father was still wallowing in his sadness, she asked desperately,

"Uma, hasn't your father got up yet? Is he still asleep?"

"If your wife has left you, what is the use of being sad about it?" That is the question she has been asking herself since yesterday. Today too she asked the same question. I suddenly replied,

"No, no. He has already got up."

I was engrossed in drawing the *kolam*. The rice flour slipped through my fingers.

"Oh, God, he's up!" Thankamani's mother went back to her house and thanked God. When I finished the *kolam*, Thambikuttan got up, came to me and rubbed his eyes. Amma's absence made no difference to him. Amma had never kept an unblinking eye on him for that. He watched me draw the *kolam*, his arms on his chin, and sat close beside me. I murmured to him.

"Is it good, Thambikuttaaa?"

With his sleepy eyes, he nodded. "Get up, let us clean and eat idly."

I rubbed the rice flour on my skirt and stood up. I held Thambikuttan by the hand and walked to the well. Even when Amma was there, I took care of him only. But today I felt a heightened sense of responsibility.

Although I was only eight years old, I understood that I had to take on the responsibility of a mother.

Together we enjoyed the breakfast that my father had prepared. He also made rice and curry for lunch. He mixed beans and yam and made a curry. It was very delicious.

While we were eating, he looked at me. Seeing his serious face, I understood the seriousness of the subject he wanted to discuss.

"From tomorrow, Achen will go to work. Uma cannot play around anymore. You will have a lot to do here."

I nodded my head in agreement. He described to me the things I should do.

"Leave Thambikuttan at Thankamani's house when you go to school. Also, you should cook rice and other dishes on the days when Achen is on day duty. It is not right to depend on the neighbours every day."

"But I do not know how to cook," I asked suddenly.

"You must learn." As he shoved the last mouthful in, he stood up. It was funny to watch him eat.

My mouth watered as he mixed the rice with the curry and balled it carefully without wasting a single grain of rice. His plate looked so clean that there was no need to wash it. He emphasized accuracy and precision in everything he did. But in his married life, he was wrong. Now I too am bearing the consequences.

Just as he had instructed me to do, I became more attentive to housework. Thanks to Thankamani's mother, I began to learn how to cook. Very quickly I learnt how to cook rice and other curries. My father was proud of me because I did my work well.

I was worried about Thambikuttan. When I finished working in the kitchen, I would feed him and take him to Thankamani's house before going to school. For two to three days this went well. On the third day, I was very disappointed when I saw how he looked when I came back from school. His body was covered with dust and dirt. Even his mouth and nose were smeared with mud. Without knowing what had happened, I looked around. Thankamani's mother frowned at me and spoke angrily.

"He does not want to obey. He would not sit quietly in one place. He's always getting into mischief."

"He's a little kid... He's old enough to play around. If you had paid attention, he wouldn't have rolled in the mud." I wanted to say those words to her, but I swallowed them.

She couldn't keep her anger under control.

"How much longer can I take care of this child? I have my own things to do. Go and tell your father to find someone else. I can't take it anymore."

"Why are you crying so much? You are standing here after eating so much earth and dust."

Sad and angry, I could not say a single word. I held him tightly by the hand and went home. I ran water over him and bathed him. His mouth was also full of mud. I tried to clean his mouth with my finger but he bit my fingers hard. I lost control of my temper and took out my suppressed anger on his tender body. My fingers left their marks on his calf. My anger increased as he cried out in pain.

As I became enraged, he cried even more. I could not bear to see the tears running down his cheeks. I hugged him tightly to my chest. When a tear fell from my eyes onto his forehead, he stopped crying and looked at me.

He saw that my eyes were moist. With his little fingers he wiped the tears away. I stood there and hugged him close to my body.

The next day I did not go to school. I stayed at home and took care of Thambikuttan. Thankamani's mother began to feel guilty. In the evening I saw her talking to my father. He consoled me.

"Maybe she was upset and said something rash. You will go to school tomorrow. She will continue to look after him."

I looked at him doubtfully.

"There is nothing else we can do." He said it calmly.

I felt that he was right. How many days could I skip school?

The next day, when I had no choice, I took him back to Thankamani's house. My head was full of worries about him. I could not sit in class in peace. After two lessons, there is a ten-minute break. When the bell rang for break, I ran home. There was a distance of almost one kilometre between the school and my house. I gathered all my strength and rushed to Thankamani's house, barely breathing.

I was relieved. He was playing in front of the house.

He was playing with a broken car and ran to me.

I stroked my fingers through his hair.

"Why did you come now? Don't you have school now?"

Thankamani's mother was not pleased to see me at this unexpected hour.

I told her that I had come for no reason and sprinted back to school. I did the same at lunch time. It was not easy for me to walk the sultry path barefoot.

When I got there, drenched in sweat, Thankamani's mother was feeding him in front of the house. I was very embarrassed. She did not like seeing me there. She brought it up quite openly.

"Why are you coming back? I am not going to hurt him."

It was not that I did not trust her. My heart was upset about Thambikuttan and I ran there to calm down. But she was hurt by it. She spoke openly to my father about it. She also gave him a little advice.

"Balan, your daughter is growing up. You are toiling day and night. It is not good to leave a grown-up girl alone."

He knows what she says is true. But he could not find a way out. She suggested something.

"Here's what you do: Let the children be at their mother's house for a while. Their grandparents are there. Let them take care of them."

He too thought that this was a good idea. He knows very well about my struggles. I felt exhausted after taking care of the house and Thambikuttan after school.

That evening when we were having dinner, Achen talked to me about it. I thought it was good when I thought of Thambikuttan. But how can I skip school? But he had found a solution.

"Let us apply for leave from school for a few days." He said. "After that, leave Thambikuttan with them and come back."

I understood that he had made his decision. Though I

was sad at the thought of leaving Thambikuttan with them and coming back, I thought it would do him good and agreed.

Amma's father, Shivashankaran Nair, was a musician. But he craved alcohol more than music, and he destroyed himself. Both grandfather and grandmother lived in Pazhayannoor with their youngest son. We hardly visited them once or twice. There was nothing or no event to remember. We walked along a path that was grassy on both sides. The granite-paved steps opened up to a large courtyard. We spotted some coconuts spread out to dry in the sun on palm leaf mats smeared with cow dung in the courtyard. A faded blue plastic net was spread over the coconuts. At one end of the mat we found a crow's feather hanging from a tapioca stalk. We stepped out onto the veranda. We did not notice anyone outside. My father knocked on the door a few times.

"Who is it?" A melodious voice came out. Thambikuttan played slinging himself on my arm. His gaze lingered on the dry paddy spikelet hanging from the roof.

"Oh, is that you, Balan? Come, children!" In a dhoti and with a towel on his shoulder, our grandfather came out. He took Thambikuttan in his arms and kissed him. He hugged me tightly and stroked my forehead.

"Sit down." He sat down on the reclining chair in the front portico, he said. My father sat down on the steel chair wired with the plastic. They both felt uncomfortable looking at each other. He asked me something to break the silence. He asked me about class, studies and so on. In pure Malayalam. Some things he asked I did not understand. But I answered as if I knew them.

"You may still be naughty..." He held his glasses on the tip of his nose and glanced over them to tease me.

I looked him in the eye. No, now his eyes did not look any different than usual. On his last visit to Sinthamanipudur, he was in for a cataract operation. His treatment was free on my father's ESI card. After that, he stayed at our house for almost a week. After the operation, his eye was bandaged. He was one-eyed like the villains in the movies.

I had a feeling that he was a real villain. This thought came to me the day he beat me up for the first time. When he entered the house, he found me arguing with my father over a glass of milk that I refused to drink. When my father accepted defeat, grandpa took up the challenge.

"Give it to me. I will make her drink it." He took the glass from my father and turned to me. I sat there wondering if he would do what my father could not. First he tried to coax me. When he realized it was not working, he tried threats. He threatened that he would beat me if I did not drink it. This made me angry. I shouted at him.

"Who are you to make me drink? Are you ready to beat me? If you hit me, I will hit you back!"

"Will you? Let me see!"

He put the glass down and jumped up to grab me. Knowing that he would win if he caught me, I ran away. I thought he could not beat me running. That was a misjudgment on my part. When I reached the second lap around the house, he had me in his arms like a little chick. While running, I did not notice the stick in his hand. I got a slap on the butt. I cried out loudly in humiliation and agony.

" If you cry, I will beat you more, you are very naughty" he said, pointing the cane at my face. As my bottom was still burning from the caning, I had no choice but to submit to him. Like an obedient child, I took the glass from him and drank the milk in one gulp. Like an act of revenge...

Although at first, we behaved like the proverbial mongoose and snake, we gradually became closer. When grandfather came back after the eye operation, I was sad. It was disheartening to see his one eye bandaged. I remembered that our science teacher had mentioned that leafy vegetables were good for eyesight. I went to the neighbour's house and got spinach and drumstick leaves for him. Then I thought about how to protect his eyesight. Now he would have thought about how to get rid of his eyesight. When we arrived, he was doubly shocked that his daughter had abandoned her unfortunate children. In his heart he was crying. He believed he was down on his luck - a heavy burden for the earth to witness such terrible events.

"I came here to leave the children for a few days. I am not in a position to take care of everything now. I have nowhere else to leave them. Let them stay here for a while. After some time, I will come back to get them."

He was very direct with his words. Grandfather wanted to say something, but he choked on his words. He only murmured in agreement.

"I am more worried about Thambikuttan. We leave him with the neighbours when I go to the mill or Uma goes to school. It is not all right. It will be fine here."

He looked at my father's face seriously for a while and then said,

"Let them be here, Balan. Let them live here. "

His words sounded hollow. As if he said them out of a sense of guilt. As if he was afraid of someone. As my father prepared to leave, he said with regret, "Grandmother seems to have gone to the temple. Please do not leave without some tea."

My father said no and got up to leave.

Though grandfather kept coaxing him to wait till grandmother came, my father did not relent. He left his leather suitcase with us. In it were some of our clothes. We had no idea what to do. We sat on the doorstep and looked at the path our father had taken.

When she came in through the back door, we did not see grandma coming. Inside the house, grandpa told her everything that had happened. When she saw us sitting on the doorstep, she came and sat next to us. She took Thambikuttan in her arms and kissed him. She stroked my hair. Her inner despair reflected in her wrinkled face. She wiped her eyes and led us into the house.

It was the grandmother who bathed Thambikuttan, fed him and took care of him. He was completely immersed in her love. I too rejoiced and thought that we had been given a new life. I even thought about why we were so late in extending our arms to this branch of love. But all these expressions of love did not last long. They ended abruptly, like a dream. I felt that grandma's love and care were just a show. But with us, grandpa became lively and cheerful. He enjoyed petting Thambikuttan and helping me study. I, who always called them *Thatha* and *Paatti* (Grandfather and grandmother), was encouraged to call them *Muthassan* and *Muthassi*(Grandfather and grandmother),. He taught us to read and write Malayalam. I learnt Shivasthuthi and Devisthuthy by heart. Grandma was more powerful in the house than Grandpa. He never felt strong enough to go beyond what Grandma said. As the days passed, Grandma started being nasty towards us. She started scolding us a lot. She used to be eager to feed us. Now she behaved as if she meant, 'Eat if you want'. She kept asking why she should be punished for the sin her daughter had committed. We spent our days not understanding whose sins we were being punished for. I was given chores like tending the barn. She found fault with me and scolded me for everything I did. Thambikuttan's situation was even more pathetic. He never got food on time. I felt that we had to return somehow. When such things happened, it looked as if grandfather would explode. But that never happened.

We stayed there for just under a month. While we wanted to go back to our father, grandma also decided to send us home. One day she woke us up early in the morning and asked us to get ready. I wanted to dance around with joy. We had been waiting so eagerly for this. She had decided to do it, at least now. I had to get Thambikuttan ready first. As I was getting him dressed after bathing, he asked,

"Are we going to Achen?"

After coming here, he often asked me when we would

return to our father, but I answered him vaguely, "We will," as I was not sure when. But this time I was able to answer him.

"Thambikuttaa... We are going back to Achen's house."

His face brightened. Memories of his father came like a cool breeze to his young mind. It gave him goose bumps. Grandfather was happier than we were. He watched our misery helplessly. "They are little children. Why are you so rude?" He asked them when his heart was broken.

"Are you still soft on them? A father who could not raise his daughter well now justifies it!" She burst into a fit of rage.

"Have you amassed enough wealth to take care of them? And look at the girl. She will grow up very quickly."

When she said that and looked at me, I wanted to ask her, "Is a girl a burden on the house and the land?" Thankamani's mother also used to say, "It is a girl. In a blink, she will grow up. Be careful."

In those moments I used to think, 'Is it a shame to be born a girl? Grandmother is a woman. Thankamani and her mother are also women. Why do they still blame women? Someone in my head is always shouting that women are the worst enemies of women.'

I packed all our clothes in a bag. I checked again to see if we had forgotten anything. Did we bring anything valuable? I looked at Thambikuttan, who was holding a small sculpture of an elephant. A wooden sculpture. It was on the table in the room. It was the only toy he found in the house. Grandmother never liked it when he took it away. She would take it away from him and scold him. Once he even got a slap in the face for it.

"No, Thambikuttaa, leave it back there."

He looked at the elephant again. Though he did not want it, he held it back. Seeing the sadness on his face, I too became sad.

"Let us ask Achen to buy a bigger elephant. This big!"

I opened my arms to show the size of the elephant.

"How am I going to hold such a big elephant?" The elephant

I showed him was not as big as he had wanted.

Grandfather sat very glumly in his chair as I walked to the portico, with the leather case in one hand and Thambikuttan in the other. He sat like an unwelcome old rag, crumpled, on the armchair. I went up to him and called out.

"Take care, Muthassaa."

His eyes were puffy and tears threatened to flow. We felt the warmth of his chest as he leaned forward and held us. Without saying a word, he blessed us with his hands on our foreheads and said goodbye.

When we left, the morning sunlight had just started drawing *kolam* in the front yard.

On the bus, enjoying the slightly warm breeze, I dozed off. Thambikuttan slept leaning on my shoulder. Grandma was sitting at the edge of the seat impassively as if she were getting rid of two kittens who had become a great nuisance to her. I woke up as the smell of the tar melting in the scorching heat pierced my nose. The nature of the heat had changed as we reached Sinthamanipudur from Pazhavannoor. Warm sunlight became scorching sunlight.

"I am not coming there. You must be knowing how to reach home from here." When the bus stopped, grandma put our leather suitcase out and asked us. It is still nearly a kilometre away from our home. She stared at me as I stood there without any reply and went on angrily,

"I must go back by the same bus; I don't have time to fret over you."

"Yes, we will go."

Grabbing Thambikuttan by the hand, who was standing stunned and drowsy, I started walking. That walk was not as easy as the race I used to make home to look after Thambikuttan.

The sun was burning brightly above our heads. As his feet scorched, Thambikuttan started whimpering.

"Come fast; it is only a little while more; walk fast." I dragged him by the arm. He sat on the road, crying and protesting that he could not walk anymore. As there was no other way, I took him up, and holding the suitcase up, I staggered on. When a horse cart passed by, I wished he would offer us a lift. That wish faded away along with the cart.

Thankamani was stirring the chillies left to dry in the sun. She ran to us as she saw us coming tired, our clothes drenched in sweat. As soon as she saw us, she took Thambikuttan on her shoulder.

"Uma," She called out with joy, more with love.

"Why did you come back? I am happy to see you. I was sad for so long. There isn't anyone to play with. It was boring, very boring."

I wanted to talk to her out of excitement at seeing her after such a long time. But being tired, I just wanted to sit somewhere. She took us to her house. I put the leather suitcase on the floor and sat on the veranda. Drenched in sweat, my frock stuck to the wall.

"Did you come alone? Didn't anyone come with you?"

Thankamani's mother asked as she came out of the kitchen, looking happy. I nodded my head, saying no. Seeing my tired face, her face changed.

"Who brought you? Why couldn't they come home and leave you here?"

So many questions in a single breath. I felt a little relieved as I drank the water that Thankamani had brought. Feeling better, I recounted everything that happened. I did not want to hide anything. I knew that she would take up the responsibility of telling everything to my father.

She didn't betray my trust. As soon as my father came,

she recounted the whole story to him, adding a little bit here and there. "Is she a woman who left two small children on the road, in the hot sun?" She kept repeating this question many times during the conversation.

"Come what may, let your children be with you. Don't send them there. They don't like the children much."

Her words touched my father's heart. He looked at her pathetically. Her anger towards grandma hadn't subsided yet.

"After all, these are her daughter's kids. Why is she so angry with them?"

My father was filled with sadness. He took Thambikuttan in his arms and kissed him on the crown. Being so happy to have seen Achen, Thambikuttan sat clasping him. He took me very close and kissed me on the cheeks.

Our reunion was very emotional. We adhered to our father like two chicks seeking protection under the wings of a mother hen. Thankamani's mother went back to her house, wiping her eyes.

SIX

Nothing has changed. What would change in a month? My father's life had become mechanical, his work shifts either all night, all day or day and night evenly divided. I had very quickly resigned myself to my old routine. I noticed from Thankamani's behaviour that my absence, even if it was brief, affected her the most. She smothered me with her love. She stayed with me most of the time.

In the height of summer, most of the wells in Sinthamanipudur had dried up. Our consolation was the water brought by trucks early in the morning. Very early in the morning I went with Thankamani to fetch water. This was the hardest task for her. Her mother took care of the rest of the work in the house. After fetching the water, I had to clean the front yard and put down the *kolam*, all by myself. Then I make the food for the morning and afternoon. After that I'll wake Thambikuttan, feed him, take him to Thankamani and then walk to school.

Now she takes more care of him. That was the only relief for me after my return from Pazhayannoor. She took care of Thambikuttan without much fuss.

But how long can this go on?

On the way to school, Hemalatha told me that a *vadhiyaar* (Brahmin teacher) came to the wedding hall to teach young children. He gathered children aged two and a half to three years to sing and play around. His wife was also there to help him. He was also an expert nagaswaram player. Short and pot-bellied. Nearly sixty years old. Though he covered his upper body with a gold-rimmed dhoti, the sacred thread stood out above his belly. But that was not the most interesting thing about him. His long nose was particularly attractive. When he played nagaswaram, we doubted whether his fingers were playing nagaswaram or his nose.

Vadhyaar and his presence proved to be a blessing, especially for us. My father too was eager to take Thambikuttan there. I took him there while he went to school. In the evening we brought him back. *Vadhyaar* was happy because he got a small amount of money at the end of every month.

Since I could not go to school for a month, I was busy most of the time. I spent more time in school copying notes and learning subjects that I would never understand on my own. KG Group owned Kathirinmel School where I studied. They also owned the mill where my father worked. The school was aimed at the children of the mill workers. Rakianna Gounder was the headmaster. He looked aristocratic. The students, teachers and locals had great respect for him. He was strict in his handling of the school. The classrooms and the school grounds had to be kept clean. Every Friday, the classes were cleaned up during the last lesson. The blackboard had to be polished dark with charcoal. Every fortnight the floor has to be rubbed with cow dung and polished. The school grounds have to be cleared of all weeds. Each class had to take responsibility for these tasks.

He justified this by saying that the sense of hygiene starts at home.

Although the class teachers led these activities, he supervised them. Since Gounder motivated them by his loving presence and commitment without intimidating them, no one found this task burdensome. He silently demonstrated how to earn love by giving it. It does not discriminate according to size, difference between owners and workers, or between rich and poor. When love and unity prevail, not only are the classrooms and school grounds clean, but so are our minds. With this, Rakianna has taught a crucial lesson that is not in the curriculum.

Every day there was a school assembly in the morning. In the morning it began with a prayer. We stood in rows and repeated the prayer after the headmaster. The headmaster and all the other teachers were present. In the evening we sang *Jana Gana Mana* and parted. If there is a serious issue, the headmaster addresses the assembly. He made exclusive speeches on Teachers' Day or Children's Day. He taught us grammar. That was only once a week. But everyone liked his lessons. He would move on to a new topic only after making sure that even Ganeshan could speak without grammatical errors. He never considered anyone worthless.

It was an unusually warm day. By the time I finished my chores, I was late.

I took Thambikuttan to *vadhyaar* and walked to school. I am used to that by now. Nowadays, I am usually late when I finish at home.

That is why Thankamani could not accompany me most of the time.

I saw a small crowd on the street and stopped. People were chatting among themselves. Curious to know what was going on, I went over to them. In the middle of the crowd, on the street, a woman was lying on the ground. She was bleeding from the forehead. People were watching, but no one went to her. They said that someone had notified the police. There was an accident - an autorickshaw collided with a bus going to Salem. The woman was sitting in the autorickshaw. For a moment I was stunned, but I took courage and went to her. There was a pool of blood around her head. I lifted her blood-soaked head into my lap. People started murmuring as I opened my school bag and dripped water into her mouth. The water dripped in through her dry lips. Squirming in pain, she tried to open her eyes but could not. Blood stained my hands as well as my skirt and blouse. In the meantime, a vehicle had arrived. Some came and lifted her into the car and took her to the hospital.

The crowd started saying something and looking at me. I ignored what these people were saying, took my bag and sprinted to the school.

After the school assembly, classes had already started.

I looked closely at my blouse and skirt. Both looked red, soaked with blood. Thinking I would be late if I washed, I ran straight to class.

It was Murugesan sir's English class. He was writing something on the blackboard and did not notice me standing at the door. The students were stunned when they saw the blood on my uniform dress. The teacher heard them murmuring and turned around. His eyes met mine as I stood at the door. He pretended to be waiting to scold me. The shopkeeper, who was in the crowd, seemed to have brought the story into the staff room. He started quizzing me as if he knew all the details.

"What is this, Uma? All of them were waiting for the police. Why are you like this?"

He spoke as if he was afraid of the consequences of my actions. I knew very well that I had done nothing wrong.

I stood there bravely, without fear.

He did not like my audacity.

"Do you think you are Mother Teresa? Born to serve the whole nation!" He mocked me. The other students started laughing at me. He looked at them sternly and reprimanded me,

"When you come to school, try to study."

I was disappointed but stood there without showing it. He looked at me again and continued.

"Go and wash off the blood. Then come to class."

I put my bag down near the door and walked to the water pipe. I smelled my hand. The raw odour of blood. First, I rubbed my palm on the floor and washed it off.

The blood stains on my clothes remained despite repeated washing. It just spread everywhere. The smell on my palms went away. I went back to the classroom. The teacher showed no mercy to me even though I was standing there wet.

"Have you washed... Stay there till the dress dries."

He wanted to punish me by keeping me outside the class.

I could not understand what I had done wrong. When the next lesson started, I went into the class.

The other students crowded around me, wanting to know what had happened. I sat huddled there without saying anything.

All the teachers had heard about the incident. It showed in their words and behaviour. But unlike Murugesan sir, no one expelled me from the class.

But their sharp words were meant to reprimand me. They frightened me. The policemen would come. I will have to make a statement. I may have to go to the police station when they call.

When the last hour was over, I felt relieved. Now no one would blame me.

The bell for the meeting rang. I went and stood in line, huddled together, not looking at anyone. Normally we chant *Jana Gana Mana* and spread out. In contrast, the headmaster's voice rose.

"Good evening, students."

I lifted my face and looked at him. He gives speeches only on special days. Is today a special day? I could not figure it out. He continued seriously.

"This school has a tradition... I have been the headmaster here for many years. Many of the students here learn well. I am happy to see them grow. I am proud and happy that I am educating students who are doing good for society."

All eyes were on the headmaster. Everyone knew what he was saying.

No one doubted Rakianna Gounder's services to the

school. Why was he mentioning them now? I waited eagerly to rush home and change my blood-stained dress.

"Something has happened in this school today that is worth celebrating... Before I announce it, I would like to invite a girl."

I too was eager to know who it was.

Who made the school proud? I raised my eyes to look at the headmaster but lowered them again when I noticed Murugesan sir looking at me.

"Uma Devi, come here."

A bee buzzed in my ears as the headmaster called me. I was stunned. Apart from me, there is no Uma Devi in the school.

"Did he call me?"

I lifted my face.

I was startled to realise that hundreds of eyes were staring at me. He was waving his hand and calling me. I tried in vain to hide my blood-stained uniform.

While holding me by his side, he continued to speak.

"Uma, from our school, created a model for humanity today. When Uma was on her way to school, she found a woman in danger. Upholding human values, she took the lead and helped her. As the result, they were able to save her life."

My fears disappeared when I heard him describe what had happened. I felt proud. I held my head high. Many eyes looked at me, filled with wonder. The headmaster touched my shoulder. He looked at me lovingly and said, "Her behaviour makes me proud and honoured. If she has the mentality at this young age to do such a good deed for others, I am very happy."

I felt like I was going to burst into tears. Hearing such good words, my self-esteem soared. I no longer bothered to hide the bloodstains on my uniform.

Let everyone see...

The headmaster pulled me close to him.

"What shall be an appropriate gift for her? For now, I would like to give her my pen."

He took out his pen from his pocket and offered it to me. Tears welled up in my eyes. Sobbing, I accepted the pen with both hands. The students burst into rhythmic applause. I held the pen close to my chest and turned around. Murugesan sir, looking me in the eye, lowered his gaze. Not only him, everyone applauded me in the same rhythm.

A Camlin pen. The very first gift in my life.

Elated with this precious gift, I held it tightly and stood beside the headmaster with my head held high.

Jana Gana Mana flowed from every throat.

My mind was full of the headmaster's words.

"We do not live here to pump more waste into the earth. When we go back, we should leave our signature somewhere. We have to leave a good lesson for the generations to come."

SEVEN

There are no wounds that time will not heal.

If my mother's departure had left a wound, time would heal that too. That was my belief. But some of the villagers, not wanting to let that happen, continued to mock me and mention it wherever they could. There was a person called Mani from Palakkad, a vicious person who wanted to add more salt to the wound. His house was the last in the same row as ours. Two other people lived there with him - Raja and Vetrivel, who were also from Tiruchirappalli.

Mani, who thought he looked more handsome and better groomed, was very pompous in his appearance.

In reality, Amma's departure did not have much impact on us. I did the same chores I used to do when Amma was with us, but now with more seriousness. The branches of my father's shame that his wife had run off with someone else also began to dry up.

In the evenings we used to play on the small street between the houses. Our gang included me and Thankamani, Shilpa and Latha who were younger than us, Thambikuttan and some other children his age. We girls played games like 'catch if you can', 'hide and seek', juggling pebbles or 'catch if you can' on one leg. The little children played ball games. As soon as the games started, we were very loud. I was always very noisy too. I never had the feminine virtues Thankamani's mother preached about. According to her, discipline and submission are the best qualities in a woman. I, who watch movies at night, climb trees and jump over walls, was supposed to be virtuous? Some even asked me mockingly, "Are you a girl?"

That day, Maniyannan asked me something that had a similar meaning. We started our games when Mani and Vetrivel were standing in their yard smoking a beedi, after their day's work at the mill.

They said something about us and laughed. This did not affect us. In the meantime, a ball thrown by Thambikuttan fell into their yard. The property wall is almost as high as a man. Without hesitation, I jumped over the wall and caught the ball. I did it so as not to spoil the fun. When Thambikuttan got the ball back, he clapped his hands and laughed. Mani gave me a wicked smile as I looked at him. He drew in a puff, looked at Vetrivel and said loudly,

"She will jump over it and more. Like mother, like daughter."

He laughed and made fun of me. Vetrivel laughed too. I kept playing because I didn't know what they were saying. But Thankamani was staring at them. Then it did not dawn on me that he had said something bad. Just before I went home, when the games were over, Thankamani explained.

"Uma, didn't you understand what he said? He said that just like your mother eloped with Palanichamy, you will elope with someone."

Thankamani, two years older than me, understood the hidden meaning very well. That was why she was staring at him. I too was angry with her.

"If you had told me about it then, I would have told him off. Then he would have been quiet."

Seeing me angry, she regretted telling me.

When she went to her house, I asked no one in particular,

"I will never elope with anyone; where will I go?"

That night I could not sleep. I lay there with my eyes closed and thought about how I could trap Mani.

Mani, Vetrivel and Raja lived in the same house but cooked separately. Mani from Palakkad did not like the dishes that others prepared. Mani cooked his own rice and curry. During my observation the next day, I noticed that Mani kept his rice to cook and then went to the well to fetch water.

The next day I got up earlier than usual. I hid outside his house. I ran into his kitchen as Mani went out with the pot to fetch water. The rice was boiling in the pot. The lid of the pot danced in the steam.

"Hey, Maniyaa, this is the punishment for you." I felt great joy at the sight of the salt crystals in my hand. I pushed aside the lid that was dancing on the boiling water. As the lid fell, the grains of rice that were about to splash out, calmed down. They made a meditative sound that sounded "Glum...Glum...".

Without wasting a single grain, I threw all the salt into the pot.

In their meditation, the grains of rice embraced them. Everything dissolved into them. I put the lid back on the pot and slipped out. I ran back home.

My joy knew no bounds. But I did not want to finish this punishment in one day. I repeated it the next day as well. Nothing changed except that I increased the amount of salt. Although I left him alone for the next two days, I went back to his kitchen on the third day. But I got caught that day.

I landed right in front of Raja, who had risen early to cook his meal. Confused, with a look that alternated between my bewildered face and the packet of salt in my hand, he asked me,

"Hey, shorty! Was that you?" He couldn't believe it.

"He's a bad guy. I can't bear to see him. Not only that; I will do more."

I said this without feeling ashamed that I had been caught.

"Because you did that, he could not even eat for the last two days. All his food is too salty. He doesn't know why. No one knows."

I was reassured. I could at least let him starve for two days. His hungry, exhausted face came to my mind.

I believed that the punishment I had inflicted on him

was not enough. But I could not escape the mocking words and looks by punishing only one Mani. Many kept repeating what Mani said.

I swore to myself that I would never run away with anyone. I argued with those who made fun of me for mentioning it. The wound my mother had inflicted on me remained for a long time.

My father was too ashamed and unwilling to visit relatives. The only relief was to visit his sister's house in Coimbatore. My aunt's son, Hariyettan, would come and take us with him. Sometimes one of his brothers from Palakkad would also come to visit us. They would bring things like jackfruit, mango or tapioca. We would then share all these with our neighbours. One jackfruit was cut into five or six pieces and divided. We took only a part of it. When they got some, they did the same. That was the Sinthamanipudur model of give and take. No one thought of keeping anything for themselves. This sense of togetherness led to a festive event every year. It was the rare event that all the families came together to turn a full moon night into a day of activities. I will tell you more about this later. Now you may be curious to know more about our new connections.

It was Sreedevi *Ilayamma* who came up with the idea. She is the wife of Achen's youngest brother.

One day, both *Ilayachen* and *Ilayamma* (father's younger brother and wife) came home. They brought a heavy parcel and placed it on the table. In a fit of emotion, they hugged both of us. They opened the parcel, took out the banana crisps and placed them in front of Thambikuttan. Achen and *Ilayachen* started talking about local events. *Ilayamma* took me to her room, combed my hair and fixed it.

"What is this, Uma? Don't you put oil before taking a bath? Look at your hair."

When the comb did not move freely between my hair

strands, she asked me. When she pulled hard, it hurt me.

"I oil myself every day."

"Then why is your hair like this?" *Ilayamma* pulled my hair together and said, "Hair makes girls look graceful."

Not discipline or submission? That's what I was going to ask. Thankamani's mother always advises that discipline and submission are the characteristics of graceful girls.

For each person, the definition of grace may be different. Or has anyone ever defined women precisely? Apart from every person putting a crown of grace or beauty on her for convenience, would she ever be able to define her own identity?

"Oh, that hurts!"

My naïve thoughts departed as it pained me when *Ilayamma* quickly pulled the comb out of my tangled hair. As I cried aloud, she reprimanded me with love.

"Does not that hurt? From now on, you must oil your hair as I tell you. Then it won't hurt."

Ilayamma took some coconut oil in her palm and massaged it into my hair. It was very soothing, the way her fingers ran through my hair. I sat there and looked at her. While she applied kohl to my eyes after bathing me, she said, "That's how it is when girls grow up alone. They would not take care of their hair. They won't use kohl. You need mothers for all that. When she is gone, can you go on as you are?"

I did not understand what *Ilayamma* was getting at. Apart from the packet of banana crisps she had brought, she had another packet in mind. This packet was meant for my father, I understood later. After putting kohl on my eyes, she took me to the veranda and said to my father,

"Look at them now."

Achen looked at me from head to toe. He was looking at his daughter who had braided her hair into a pigtail and rimmed her eyes with kohl.

He was probably smiling with pride, but I am not sure. He knew very well that I like to braid my hair and line my eyes with kohl. He had tried his hand at it many times but failed. *Ilayachen*, looking at me with a certain composure, smiled too.

"We have come to discuss something important. Balettan must agree with us." *Ilayamma* opened what was on her mind. My father stared at her, not understanding anything.

"The girl is known to me. She is uneducated. And what has education got to do with it?"

Ilayamma was tremendously adept at keeping people on their toes.

"Who are you talking about?"

But Achen played the spoilsport. *Ilayamma* was forced to cut the story short without stretching it any further.

"It's about you, Balettan."

She pressed me against her and continued in a somber tone.

"There should be someone to take care of the children. You may not need a partner. But these children should not grow up like this."

Did my father's heart waver at the seriousness of my *Ilayamma*? I felt it. I felt that what *Ilayamma* said was appealing. I put my arms around her neck and stood close to her.

"It wouldn't work anymore. They will grow up well. I will

take care of them."

With a distant look, he conveyed his firm resolve. *Ilayamma*'s face turned grim.

"I have said what came to my mind. The rest is in your hands."

She took me by the hand and went inside. She sank me deep into temptation.

"Uma, she is nice. If she comes here, she will comb your hair like this every day. She will put kohl on your eyes. Talk to your father."

I nodded my head.

She was a relative of *Ilayamma*. Twenty-seven years old. For some reason she did not marry. Nor did they have the financial means to pay a dowry. *Ilayamma* felt unhappy in her plight and probably suggested this. But my father was not willing. *Ilayachen* also tried to change his mind. I took it upon myself to emerge victorious if they were defeated. In the days that followed, my behaviour worried him. I, who usually cooked rice and other dishes with enthusiasm, was now very reserved. He understood me when I started showing less interest in taking care of Thambikuttan as well. But to understand what was going on, he asked.

"What happened to you, Uma?"

At first, I avoided him. He came to me, put his arm on my shoulders and asked me again. I wanted to broach the subject before he got upset. I said, not missing the serious tone,

"Let us go to Sreedevi *Ilayamma*. Let us meet the person she mentioned." I said feeling that I had almost completed my mission. He stepped closer to me and with a more serious look than before, declined my offer.

"Uma, this might not work. I am not sure she will take good care of both of you. We will lose the peace we have now."

I felt like crying. *Ilayamma* had said she would braid my hair. She will put kohl in my eyes. Then how can it be that she will not take care of us? My father has only lame excuses. In my helplessness, I was at my wits' end when I said,

"Should not I study? Should I not go to school? Shall I keep looking after Thambikuttan and keep cooking the food?" I continued bitterly. I looked at him furtively. It was a brahmastra.

I felt it pierce his heart. He looked a little touched. He got up and left without a word. In the following days he seemed thoughtful.

On Sunday morning, we started our journey to Palakkad. We took the transport bus that went from Coimbatore to Palakkad. We had the rare opportunity to see our father's bride-to-be. We both sat in the front row with our father, right behind the driver. Thambikuttan, who did not understand that he would see his father's new bride, was happy about the ride. From Palakkad we have to walk ten minutes to reach Kaadambuzhakkonam, where his ancestral home is located. From the main road, we walk along a small path lined with lush green trees. The feeling of being in search of the greatest happiness of my life spurred me on. My feet gained speed. Thambikuttan's legs protested after walking for some time. Achen took him on his shoulders. He sat upright and smiled as if he was sitting on an elephant.

Ilayamma was happiest to see us. She, who was fetching water from the well, put the bucket down near the well and ran to meet us. She took Thambikuttan in her arms.

She touched my chin and congratulated me, almost saying, "Smart girl, you did it." I got goosebumps from her cold and wet fingers.

Ilayamma, Ilayachen and an elderly uncle came with us to see the bride. We took a bus from my father's ancestral home. I heard *Ilayamma* telling her neighbour that we were going to see the girl from the tea shop. Whatever the shop was, I was eager to see her. Sreedevi *Ilayamma* was our team leader. The family is known to her. They are not only known, they are distant relatives.

This marriage proposal also reflected *Ilayamma*'s concern for a family that is not doing well financially. Sreedevi *Ilayamma* was sure that my father, with a fixed income, would be a support for her, even though this would be his second marriage.

As soon as I entered her house, I started watching her.

The bride-to-be was taller than my father. She is fair and slim built. But she looked beautiful. Her smile caught my eye at first sight. The rest went like a dream. She sat me close to her and braided my hair into a pigtail. She lined my eyes with kohl. She took Thambikuttan into the house and fed him. She held me close and asked me many questions.

"Did you like your *Memma* (Mother's sister)?"

My eyes fell out of my head when she asked this question. I looked at her in amazement and thought: Should I call her *Memma*? As if she understood me, she said,

"You may call me *Memma*, both of you". She kissed Thambikuttan, her lips lightly brushing his cheek. He screwed up his face as if he did not like it.

"I like you." I croaked, touching her palm.

As we finished the traditions of viewing the bride-to-be and got up to go on our way, *Memma* held me again and stroked my back. In her arms I found a place of refuge. My heart was pounding very fast.

I conceded her my mother's place, but my father was as hesitant as the monsoon clouds that did not know whether to rain or not. I kept describing her until we returned to Sinthamanipudur. I told Achen that from the moment I saw her, I thought of her as my mother.

"Uma, there is no one like one's mother. Whatever her weaknesses, only the mother who gave birth to you will understand you and your pains." Like a philosopher, he said.

In my mind, I said, my father, who has known the cruelties of stepmothers by reading or seeing, has a flawed understanding.

"*Memma* is good, better than Amma." Achen never thought I would ever say that.

Though he wavered, two external factors forced my father to decide to remarry. Thankamani's mother was one of them. She came in the guise of a counsellor. As usual.

"Balaa... When children grow up, they need support. Get married, no doubt. She will be a help to you in your old age." Achen sat like an obedient lamb.

The second reason was an emotional one.

There was a letter from our grandfather in Pazhayannoor. He changed his mind.

"Let me write this letter with an apology. I beg your forgiveness for the wrong my daughter has done to you. I would have liked to take care of your children. But I am no longer able to do so. But when they came to stay with us for a few days, I was very pleased. But you know the situation here...."

This showed his utter helplessness.

In the last paragraph he wrote as follows:

"Your children need a mother. By your care alone it may not be possible to bring them up to be wise children. Consider this my request, and marry again. Live comfortably. I want to close my eyes after seeing this. With love, Shivashankaran Nair."

Grandfather vented his guilt and regret in this letter. Each sentence was strong enough to change my father's mind. Like everyone else, he too was concerned for our safety. Especially because I am a girl.

The whole of society is concerned about a woman's safety.

But where would a woman find safety?

Such anxious thoughts began to rise in my father too. Before the aftershocks could subside, he made this decision. This beautiful, slender woman enters my life. The shadows of neglect that haunted my life because my mother left would end. The taunts that came from many would cease. A mother comes to bring in the cool breeze of love.

I must lie in the curve of her arms and lean my head against her bosom. In the nights that followed, I dreamed of *Memma*.

EIGHT

Who decides the course of our lives? Is it God? How then can we say that our lives belong to us?

My father's second wedding was held at the Cherpulassery Krishna temple. It was an ordinary wedding without any pomp, with very few guests. I went around holding *Memma*'s hand. Even when we came to our house in Sinthamanipudur after the wedding, I stood there in full splendor holding her hand. I wanted to show off in front of the people who were taunting us. I played the good hostess and served water and tea to the neighbours who had come to see the new bride. They all said the same thing.

"What Balan has done is right. After this, the children would feel the love of their mother. And that is a security for them."

So many hearts were worried for us who were growing up without our mother's love. Some others looked happy as if they had read my mind.

"Uma, now you are accepted. Don't worry about your younger brother in the future. Your mother will take good care of him. You will also become happy."

I too thought the same thing. But the person who wrote my destiny calculated something more accurate. These calculations would never go wrong, even when adding, subtracting, dividing or multiplying.

The crowd and the noise were over. The celebrations ended. The sun rose as it always does in Sinthamanipudur. Like a wound-up alarm clock, I got up early the next day and started my morning work. I filled the pots with water. I cleaned the front courtyard and painted *kolam* there. To prove my cooking skills before *Memma*, I made idly, sambar and chutney. I was unusually enthusiastic. I thought she would judge me by what I did and I was very careful about every task. I bubbled over with joy as I imagined *Memma*, the judge, congratulating me.

I had done nothing wrong.

"How did you learn to prepare these dishes?' She asked as she took breakfast. '"It is very tasty. Our chutney is not like that. It is rather watery." *Memma* enjoyed the thick chutney and said.

"The traditions in Tamil Nadu are a little different. Not like in Palakkad." Achen ate along with *Memma* and said.

"Little Uma is the one who does everything here. So, she knows it all. Right, Uma?"

I smiled. I was proud and stood tall. *Memma* took the opportunity.

"It will take some time for me to get used to your habits." While clearing the plates, she smiled furtively at my father and said. He looked at me as if he had a guilty conscience and kept his head down.

I woke up Thambikuttan, fed him and had breakfast too. I felt that I had never prepared a tastier meal.

I also made lunch for that day. Not just that day. It is better to say every day. *Memma* used the excuse that she did not know our habits. She never used what she knew, nor did she try to learn ours. After two days, Achen started going to his work. And I to school after the days of leave I had taken to attend my father's wedding.

Nothing changed in our house except that we had an extra member to share the limited resources. My daily routine continued. I continued to do the housework and look after Thambikuttan.

"I don't know how to make food like Uma does."

While she continued to read magazines like Mangalam and Manorama and comic strips like Bobban and Molly that she brought from home, she urged me to do the housework. It was a mistake of mine to think that my burden would lessen when *Memma* came, but now my work has doubled.

I used to wash the dirty clothes of the three of us and

put them in the sun before going to school. Since *Memma* came, a saree has also been added. I, three feet tall, in a saree six cubits long, swayed as if I were trapped in a deep, unfathomable gorge. Helplessly, I mentioned that this task was not easy, and *Memma* took a cursory note.

"Oh, it's nothing. You would learn it like this. You too are a girl. Soon you will be wearing a saree."

Throwing her sarees in different colours in the wash, *Memma* said. Neither the colours nor her words could excite me. My life had become monotonous. Every day became more difficult. The chores at home, taking care of Thambikuttan, washing clothes and my school. I was getting very tired of everything. It was too late when I realized that my hopes that she would at least be nice to Thambikuttan had also been dashed. Achen's life revolved around his various duties at the mill and the additional work as a compounder. Did he think *Memma* was taking great care of our needs? I could not bring myself to tell Achen that the reality was different.

He had already warned me that a stepmother would always be a stepmother.

The only break from the pressures of everyday life were our visits to our aunt in Coimbatore. Every two to three weeks, Hariyettan would come with his Hercules bicycle. He always came on Friday evenings. He pedalled hard while Thambikuttan sat in front and I on the pillion. We returned on Sunday evening. Hariyettan is eight years older than me. His mother is my father's sister. My aunt has four children. Hariyettan is the eldest son. Since he is my cousin, his rights over me have been recognized by both families and other relatives.

In her house, *Ammayi* (aunt) has two milk cows and seven to eight chickens. There is milk, eggs and curd in abundance in her house. Her care was always very pleasant. *Ammayi* liked to take care of Thambikuttan. He likes it too.

She finds time to comb and braid my hair or pluck the lice off my head.

As soon as *Memma* came, Hariyettan reduced his visits to only every two or three months. *Memma* was the reason for *Ammayi* and Hariyettan's withdrawal from our lives. I realized this very late.

Memma always wanted me to be at home. After I had done all my chores, I never had time to play. She always found excuses to keep me at home. In my helplessness, I obeyed her.

I could not bear what *Memma* said almost three months after

she had come, when I was on my way to school after getting Thambikuttan.

"Why do you want to go to school? Why can't you study from home? There are hundreds of things to do at home."

"Now I have done all my chores. What is left?"

I stood there wondering what I had forgotten.

"Oh, not now. But it does not look like you will be able to go to school in six to seven months." With a heavy tone she went in.

What will go wrong after six to seven months? I had no clue about it. Because if I keep thinking about it, I will be late for school, I grabbed Thambikuttan's hand and ran. Poor Thambikuttan. He too has started running fast. His childhood is so meaningless. Are there happy moments too? Is our father able to give him warmth and comfort? These thoughts were running through my mind.

That evening, when I returned from school, it was Thankamani who told me.

"Hey, Uma, another member is coming to your home."

"My home...? Who's the new one coming...? Without my knowledge..." I looked at her doubtfully. I felt shy as she said it in a low tone.

"Your *Memma* is pregnant. Another brother or sister will come to your house."

I felt jealous of her thinking of how she knows things so well. She tells me everything that goes on at home without missing any detail.

I looked at her angrily. She returned the glance, puffed up in her pride that she knew what was coming.

Then I understood why *Memma* said that I would not be able to go to school after six to seven months. She would need someone to take care of the child and do the housework. That was what she was after.

I started to get angry with myself.

The days and months passed relentlessly, adding to my burden. *Memma's* mood swings due to pregnancy changed her behaviour. She blamed me for everything. She stopped liking the food I cooked. She started scolding me. It became even more unbearable when she insisted on switching off the light at eight o' clock. This harsh punishment came whenever I sat down to study at home after finishing work. Since I had no other choice, I went out and sat under the streetlight to study. One day when my father returned from his night duty, I was sleeping outside on the veranda, *Memma* had switched off the lights, locked the doors and was sleeping inside. When he saw me sleeping on the bare floor, he asked why. In my sleep I babbled something. He believed what *Memma* said.

"She was walking around at dusk. She will not come even if it is night."

Though it was an outright lie, my father believed it and gave me a piercing look. I sobbed, unable to convince him of my innocence.

"*Memma* turned off the lights. I went out to study."

"Finish your studies early. If you keep playing, then too... Can she wait here with the lights on?"

I realized then that *Memma* was pretty good at lying. He went in silently. Even in his silence he said what he wanted and I understood. The sentence he said when I forced him to marry *Memma* was, "No one can take the place of a mother. A stepmother will always be a stepmother."

As for me, I have nothing from my mother to be proud of or even sad about. What happy moment remains from my childhood? In my childhood, only dark clouds ever appeared.

When *Memma*'s relatives came to take her to her parents in her seventh month of pregnancy, she decided not to go. The loving *Memma* was praised by Sinthamanipudur for her magnanimity towards us. The consensus in the village was that she thought we would be miserable without her. They felt that *Memma* cared for us like the apple of her eye. In the ninth month, when she was going to her house to deliver, *Memma* hugged me tightly, which was unusual. She kissed Thambikuttan incessantly. Our neighbours who came to see her off stood stunned.

Another girl was born to my father. After the thread ceremony was over on the twenty-eighth day, *Memma* came back to Sinthamanipudur. My bad days began again. As the number of members increased, my responsibilities at home also increased.

But I firmly believed that there would be a way out of a difficult situation, however difficult it might be. I did not allow hard work, negligence or crises to affect my studies. When I reached the tenth grade, *Memma* became pregnant again. Earlier, there was an argument between Achen and *Memma* about it. At that time, Achen insisted that she should stop having children.

"I want to have a boy too." *Memma*'s words were adamant.

"We have one son, that's enough." My father's response

was pragmatic. But *Memma* tried to give it an emotional dimension.

"It is you who have a son, not me. I want to have a boy myself."

At that moment I understood what he was saying about stepmothers. A woman is sincere only to the seed that germinates within her. From *Memma*'s point of view, is it not right to ask how Thambikuttan and I, without any blood relation to her, can be her children?

God's wishes were not as *Memma* had planned them. Another girl was born to her. This time she did not go home for the delivery. After the baby was delivered in a hospital in Coimbatore, some relatives from her house came to help her, but they returned after ten days. My responsibility grew.

Even Thankamani, who understands my situation very well, started grumbling. I did not wait to explain things to her because her complaints and protests would not last long.

After quite some time, Hariyettan came home. This was unexpected and I was quite excited. Maybe for two days. I wanted to go to *Ammayi*'s house and rest. When I saw him, I ran to him excitedly. He came in and put his bike on the stand.

"We do not see much of you today, Hari."

Ilayamma, who was inside feeding the baby, came out and enquired.

"I am very busy these days. I come home very late."

He sat down on the railing of the veranda and narrated. The baby in *Memma*'s arms smiled at him, showing its toothless gums. Hariyettan stood up and took the baby from her. I made tea for him. Thambikuttan sat down close to Hariyettan. *Memma* went in to put the baby to sleep.

"Let us go." Asked Hariyettan after drinking the tea and looking at me. In the meantime, *Memma* had come out.

I nodded in agreement. As I went in to pack some clothes for me and Thambikuttan, I heard them talking to each other.

"Hari, don't think badly of me. Now she is no longer a little girl. It is not right of you to go around with her on a bicycle." *Memma*'s indifferent voice hurt him.

"It's not the first time... And am I a stranger?"

What *Memma* said was not an answer to the two questions that rose from the wounded heart.

"This is not the way we behave in our place. That's why I was just saying that you should not cycle to Coimbatore with that girl at this late hour."

I felt sad and angry at the same time. I threw down my clothes and sat on the floor. I ran out when I heard the bicycle moving from the stand. Hariyettan waved his hand at Thambikuttan and disappeared into the distance while furiously pedalling his bicycle. While my eyes filled with tears, he disappeared from my sight.

That day I felt that it was my mistake not to say anything to my father. I did not feel like complaining to him because I had vehemently urged him to have a second marriage. That was the fact. As time went by, *Memma* tried to distance us from Achen too.

"Is this how you behave towards your father? You are growing up. You are not a little girl to lean on your father's shoulder."

I did not understand her argument that you cannot even talk to your father because you are a girl.

"He is your father, not your lover."

At one point she scolded me out of earshot as I entered the house and clung to my father.

I began to get the feeling that *Memma* saw me as a burden. That could be why she found fault with everything I did. But I decided not to hide what she had said to Hariyettan.

It was only the next morning that I was able to tell my father all my grief. My father understood the gravity of the situation. He had an animated discussion with *Memma*.

"Hari has come for her, has not he? Why did you speak to him so harshly?"

"Are you blaming me for this? I was against him taking the girl in the evening. I only said that for the sake of your daughter." *Memma* was trying to change from a stepmother to a loving, sincere mother. But Achen was not convinced this time.

"There's nothing to it. For so long it was he who took the children. What would he have thought?"

Because she was being reproached, she changed her position.

"I have nothing more to say. You and your daughter can sort it out yourselves. I didn't mean to be biased. That's the only mistake I made."

Memma was acting very well. But she ended her part with a foreshadowing.

"Let me tell you something very clearly. One day you will regret his coming and going."

I didn't understand anything anymore. Why should Achen regret the arrival of Hariyettan? What was going on in her mind?

Anyway, her game was not working. Achen reiterated his point that she was in the wrong in this matter. I was comforted by his reply. I knew then that I should have told him the things that had happened earlier.

It was only after a long time that Hariyettan visited us next.

That too only at my father's insistence. *Memma* surprised us with her behaviour. Unusually, she behaved very close to Hariyettan.

From then on, Hariyettan visited our house now and then, bringing books and magazines for *Memma*.

He lost interest in taking us with him. I did not find it strange when Thankamani's mother mentioned that he

came even when we were not at home.

"Your cousin keeps coming to your house. Even this morning. He came this morning too. I have a feeling..."

She paused halfway, as if she did not want to continue. I was also surprised at the change in Hariyettan's behaviour. He no longer spoke to us — me and Thambikuttan — as he used to. I consoled myself with the thought that these changes were due to time.

It was a holiday for me, just before the annual exams. Thambikuttan was at school. Achen had gone to the mill at eleven o, clock as he was on half-night duty. I finished my chores for the day and started studying. Whatever happened at home, I never neglected my studies. I got good marks in all subjects. While I was memorizing the lessons, *Memma* came to me. Her voice was unusually soft.

"Uma, let us go to the river in the afternoon. There are some clothes to wash."

I lifted my eyes from my book and looked at her. I was surprised to see her smile. The smile we saw when we went bride-seeking for my father. I wanted to ask her where that smile had been hiding since then But I wasted no time and agreed with her.

Around twelve o, clock we went to the river. *Memma* carried the bundle of dirty clothes. I followed her.

Clear blue sky.

There was not even a cloud.

The sun has started pouring its heat on the earth to take revenge.

We walked along the burnt path. When we reached the riverbank, it waited eagerly for the benevolence of the clouds.

Despite the low water level, the river was flowing very fast. I walked along the steps to go down the embankment. *Memma* was right behind me.

"Oh, my bad memory, I forgot to take the children's clothes. While you are washing these, I will collect them and come back."

I thought this was a trick of hers to get me to wash all the clothes and laughed inwardly.

I was alone on the river bank. I went into the water.

It felt good to get my feet wet. I bent down, took water in my palms and washed my face. Both my eyes and my mind felt refreshed.

In a split second, I was startled.

It was as if the earth gave way beneath my feet. The undercurrent was too strong to gauge. Quickly the water washed into my eyes. With all my strength I tried to stay afloat. It did not work. The sandy hollow at the bottom of the river gave way under the current. I lost my grip.

When I opened my eyes, I found myself in the hospital. The rest was hearsay. Those who came and herded pigs had saved me. People deciphered things when they said another woman was with me.

They thought *Memma* had gone home while I was drowning and did not even cry for help. When they got home, *Memma* was there. Their doubts grew when they saw that Hariyettan was there too. People noticed his frequent, untimely visits to our house.

They acted without wasting a moment.

They did not even wait for my father to come home after duty, but got a taxi to take *Memma* back home. Though she kept protesting her innocence, they sent Hariyettan in the same car.

This was the beginning of a new journey in her life.

I was lying in bed in the hospital with my eyes closed. My father squeezed my right hand, sat there and cried.

Is cruel fate pulling its strings on us? I do not know. Silence flooded the words I knew. I closed my eyes tightly.

NINE

Another time of trial came to an end. Our family also came to rest, like a troubled and restless sea coming to rest. My family, consisting of Achen, Thambikuttan and me, began to live again as in our earlier days. I was the one who felt the happiest after surviving the trials by fire. Since *Memma* came, life has been quite stifling. Those two eyes just stared at me to find a flaw and scold me. I was relieved when the stale air in the house was dispelled - and I was excited. I could be free with my father. No controlling or reprimanding.

Sinthamanipudur did not change at all. The only change was the new postmaster who was transferred here. The postmaster, who came with his family from Mayiladuthurai, Kumbakonam, became the new resident of Sinthamanipudur. They were Tamil Brahmins. The postmaster was quite a reserved person. Ascetic in appearance. His family members were not often seen outside either.

I once mentioned the peculiarity of Sinthamanipudur. Let me begin there.

Just as the line houses of the lineage had no boundaries or dividing walls, neither were their minds divided. We lived like one family, sharing everything we had and loving each other.

The full moon nights are festive in the houses of Sinthamanipudur. Especially for the women.

Each kitchen prepared a special dish. The women competed with each other to make it as tasty as possible.

I was also busy with similar preparations that day. Early in the morning, Thankamani was eager to know what I would prepare. She asked me the same thing when we went to fetch water.

"Hey, Uma, what special thing do you want to do today?"

I looked at her and smiled. I tried to lift her spirits by keeping the tension up.

"I am not going to tell you right now. It's a big secret. You will be amazed once I do it."

She lost her temper.

"Oh, are you the great chef?"

She started walking faster. I let her go because I knew how far she would go if she was angry with me. After three or four steps, she stopped because I did not catch up with her.

When I caught up with her, she said with a smile,

"My mother will make *pulisadam* (tamarind rice)."

I also smiled at her. This is Thankamani. She cannot hide anything.

The full moon was coming. The earth and the moon looked at each other. They courted each other.

We celebrated *Nilasadam* on the vast sandy banks of the Sinthamani River. We gathered with the special dishes prepared in each house.

I made *thakkalisadam* (tomato rice). This is boiled white rice sautéed with green chilies, cashews, tomatoes, turmeric and ghee. Thankamani's mother is my guru in cooking. She has never been stingy with her words of praise about my cooking. "She does everything exactly the way I tell her to. And she has this innate ability to make any dish palatable." I, too, enjoy it when she flatters my cooking.

Thankamani's family brought *pulisadam* (tamarind flavored-rice), as she had mentioned in the morning. Coriander rice came from Ponnaiyyan. Curd rice, fried lentils, lemon rice, *puliogare* (tamarind rice), etc. Many special dishes came from different houses in Sinthamanipudur and were spread on Palmyra leaves. Lured by the fragrance, the waves of the river rippled.

In the moonlight, the Sinthamani River participated in our *Nilasadam* celebrations in its silver garb.

We turned night into day with songs, dances and a variety of foods.

All the families of the village enjoyed the festivities. I noticed the absence of one family. The postmaster's family.

Although it has been months since he came to the village, there is no one close to them.

But shouldn't they at least have been present on such occasions? Why didn't they join us? I enjoyed the festivities and thought that they were nothing unusual.

It was the Sunday after the full moon. Certain unusual things were happening.

I usually wake up at five in the morning to the sound of the mill siren. Nature should be kind enough to stir up earlier on some days. I don't have an alarm clock or a watch to awaken me and check the time. To get up early, I have to feel the urge to pee. Muthu's great-grandmother had told me that all you have to do to get this urge is to drink a lot of water before going to bed. I have tried that many times, and it's worked. Especially when *Memma* was with us. I used to stir up early to finish my studies before running errands at home.

On Sunday morning, I felt a similar urge and woke up early. When I went out, it was still dark. None of the houses, including ours, had a toilet. We used the riverbanks or secluded places to answer nature's call.

Just behind our house we had an enclosure near the drain. When it is very urgent, we use this area to relieve ourselves. I went there in the dark to relieve myself.

As I stood up, I heard someone drawing water, and I focused my ears on the sound. The noise was coming from the postmaster's house. I was afraid of the dark, although there was nothing to be afraid of in Sinthamanipudur.

It is the sound of running water. Who is that, in the middle of the night? I was all ears.

It was not just a feeling. It's someone taking a bath. Although my whole body began to shake, I moved closer to see better.

Although it was dimly lit, I could tell it was a woman.

A woman, with a shaved head, taking a bath. I could only see her from behind. She was covering herself from her chest to her knees. I don't remember that there were women with shaved heads in the village. Even in the postmaster's house, I have never seen anyone with a shaven head.

Then who is it?

Venkadapathi sir said in class that there are no ghosts or apparitions. And I believed it.

Nevertheless...now!

The ghosts and evil spirits I had read about in the stories flashed through my mind. I looked around. I thought something was moving in the darkness. No, there wasn't. I just had a feeling.

The sounds at the well stopped. I went on to look again. No one was there anymore. My arms and legs were shaking. Eerie thoughts were running through my head. I ran into the house without looking back and closed the door. I lay down and kept my eyes tightly closed. I felt as if someone was drawing water. I hid my face under my pillow.

I spread out my questions in front of my father, who came back from his night duty.

"Is it true that there are no ghosts or evil spirits?"

"What happened to you? ... Asking about ghosts early in the morning. Did something scare you during the night?"

Without saying yes or no, I repeated my question.

"Achen, tell me first. There are no ghosts, are there?"

I want to believe it.

I will not be relieved until he confirms it.

He answered me casually as he changed his clothes.

"Ghosts and evil spirits exist only in stories. But you have to be careful of people. Maybe you got scared that night because you read something."

He teased me, pinching my cheeks as he went to take bath with his towel.

"Ghosts...early in the morning. Old enough to be married. And her fears are growing!"

I, too, felt he had a point with his teasing.

As a small child, I used to watch movies alone at night. Where did the new fears emanate from?

But it was not just a feeling. I heard it.

I saw a woman with a shaved head with my own eyes.

That night I went to sleep very late. I tossed and turned in bed and could not sleep. I listened eagerly for sounds in the silence.

Only my breath made noise. Some time later I was startled by the grinding sound of the pulley on the well. Without making a sound, I went there. Just like the previous night.

Repetition: the same figure A woman with a smooth head pouring water over herself.

Although the darkness was frightening, I refused to give in.

I walked towards the well. I stubbed my toe on a granite stone in the darkness. It hurt. I ignored it and kept walking. Stealthily, I reached the well. I opened my eyes wide and watched cautiously.

It was not a ghost or an apparition, but a human being. A girl with a shaved head. She looks to be fifteen or sixteen years old.

She has a saffron coloured cloth draped over her chest. She shivered as the cold water flowed over her body.

I stood there transfixed.

Who is she?

I could not restrain my curiosity.

'Who are you?"

She turned to me and looked at me, stunned, as she bent down to soap her legs. She opened her mouth to scream when she saw me. I approached her and spoke in a calm voice.

"Don't be afraid. I am Uma, the compounder's daughter."

I forced her to stay as she frightenedly tried to run away. I thought she would scream in her fear.

To calm her down, I repeated my name and that I was the compounder's daughter.

She begged me while trying to control her sobbing.

"Please don't tell anyone you saw me. I am the postmaster's younger sister. I should not show myself in public. I am not supposed to talk to anyone. That's why I take a bath at night without anyone seeing me."

Her words expressed her hidden sorrow. Her tears mixed with the drops of water that stuck to her face.

I did not understand what she was saying. I did not have the words to comfort her. I stood still for a moment.

Instead of comforting words, more doubts arose in my mind.

"Why don't you come out? Why did you shave your head?"

"It's getting late; please leave. If anyone sees me, it will be a problem."

She quickly washed the soap off her body, took her change of clothes and went on her way. As she walked, she muttered in a low voice.

"Don't tell anyone you saw me."

Stunned, I watched the girl's shock and sadness and stood there for a while.

I received no answers to the questions I asked her. The same questions came back to my mind. I held on to the company of the darkness and walked back to my house. The night is still long. I quietly entered the room, rolled back into bed and pulled the sheet over my head.

Although I felt like waking my father up that very night to tell him the scenario, I decided to wait until morning.

What if he scolds me for being out in the dark all alone?

No, he knows me very well. Until morning, the stubbed toe continued to burn.

While we ate our breakfast of cooked semolina, I described the events to him.

My first-hand account of events surprised him.

"A shaved woman? In the postmaster's house?"

"Hey, I asked you yesterday about ghosts and evil spirits. That was because I saw her."

I recounted everything from the first moment. As his interest grew, I became more and more excited. I threw at him all my questions that she had left unanswered.

"Why is her head shaved? Why did she tell me not to talk to anyone about her?"

My father understood the seriousness of the situation, but said nothing. He repeated what she had also said,

"Don't tell these stories to anyone."

That day I knew he had decided to do something when he took a leave of absence from his duties at the mill. He rarely took a leave. I was always very happy on such days. I did not have to prepare food early in the morning. That day, too, I was relieved and went to school.

"Hey, Thankamani," I called out to her.

She answered as if I wanted to tell her something important. I walked close to her.

"Do you know the postmaster?" For a moment I forgot that both Pappathi and my father had told me not to tell anyone. Besides, it's Thankamani I am talking to.

She cannot keep anything in her heart. If she comes to

know about it, she will tell the whole village. With the same curiosity, she urged me to continue.

"Tell me, tell me, what is the matter with the postmaster?"

Suddenly I remembered the girl's face. Her pitying look appeared before my eyes. I changed the subject.

" Not much... That postmaster, you know, has a temper. I can't stand him."

Thankamani became angry. She must have understood that I was trying to tell her something else.

"Get lost, you shorty! You are hiding something from me."

Because it was easy to change her mind, I feigned anger.

"There's nothing else. It does not matter. Come with me."

I looked at her out of the corner of my eye. Her face was indignant.

In the evening, the postmaster always went to the Mariyamman temple. That day, when he went to the temple, my father followed him closely.

Since he was not friendly to anyone, he also ignored my father. Achen remained silent and was with him when he came out of the temple after prayers. When they reached the banyan tree, Achen called him from behind.

"Sir,"

He turned around. There was not even a trace of a smile on his face. He looked at my father inertly. In a mild tone he said, "I would like to talk to you."

He looked around. Finding no one watching, he paused, as if thinking, what is there to talk about?

" Sir, I have been watching you for some time. No one from your house approaches or interacts with anyone outside the house. Not even talking to others. No one is even seen outside."

My father paused in between looking him in the eye. His

expression did not change. He became impatient, as if he had no time to talk.

"Balaa…, You said you wanted to talk about something. Please tell me."

Achen was surprised that he addressed him by name. He knows people, though he doesn't talk to anyone. He made sure no one was around them, lowered his voice and said,

"Sir, don't hide anything from me. Last night my daughter was talking to your sister."

The serious expression on his face gave way to one of exasperation.

He looked around and said,

" Balaa…, I know about it too. My sister told me. She had problems in the place where she lived. That's why she's with me now. I should not have any problems here either. Please do not tell anyone."

With moist eyes he said this and folded his hands. He was pleading. For his sister's sake.

Achen took him home. I was amazed to see the postmaster's eyes and face, red and puffy from crying, in contrast to his stern look, as if he had been stung by a bee. As I stared at him, he beckoned me over.

"Uma,"

His voice was brittle.

I stepped closer to him.

"Don't let anyone outside know that you met and spoke with my sister. Otherwise, I will have to leave this village."

I saw that a sea of sadness was raging in his heart. Trying to control his pain, he said.

"My sister's name is Maka. She got married last year during Pongal. The groom's name was Rama Moorthy. He worked as an accountant in a tire factory. She had a happy life. But what was she to do? It was her destiny."

His words broke off. He wiped his tears with his left

hand and was silent for a moment. I looked at him and at my father. My heart was also filled with sorrow. Without looking at either of us, he continued.

" One day, when he was on his way to work, there was a serious bus accident. He was hit badly. Lost a lot of blood. He died on the way to the hospital. After that, my sister..." He sobbed and covered his face with his hands like a child, unable to finish his words. I, too, felt like crying.

My father tried to comfort him by stroking his shoulder. He wiped his face with the tip of his dhoti.

"After that, according to the customs of our community, she had to wear white clothes, shave her head and sit at home. .... She was not to come out on occasions. ... Whether good or bad, if anyone sees her in these clothes, they will rebuke her and say that this is a bad omen."

A community that sees widows as bad omens. It is so terrible to sacrifice one's life within the four walls of a house.

While listening to his voice, the images of Ponnammal selling vegetables in a white sari and Sarasu Akkal from the neighbouring village came to my mind.

They were very old. Is the young Maka like that too? How can she, who is two or three years older than me, spend her whole life in a dark room? How will she live without seeing anyone and without breathing fresh air?

A landslide of questions.

"We are from Mayiladuthurai." He didn't finish speaking. "There we had relatives living around us. Still, they would not talk to my sister. Even my children were not allowed to talk to her. So, I brought her here with me."

His words illustrated how unbearable the words of sarcasm and neglect they experienced from their relatives were. The helplessness of running away from your hometown.

Now no one knows anything about them. The request

not to disturb the peace. That is what he is repeating. I felt he was a little relieved after telling the story.

"I need to see Maka."

I decided. He did not deny it. Maybe he was looking forward to it, too. He walked ahead of us. I followed my father.

In addition to Maka, the family included the postmaster's wife and two children. As soon as she saw us, she hid behind the door. Only after he had explained everything, she was ready to face us. Shadows of fear also appeared on her face. I felt that her house was filled with fear.

The master's wife led me to Maka's room.

When I entered the room, I felt suffocated. The postmaster's wife lit a kerosene lamp in the room. In its dim light, I saw Maka lying on the bed, facing the wall, and was shocked. When the light of the lamp filled the room, she stood up, startled. I saw her pale face. Like a sunflower wilted without sunlight.

I let my eyes glide over the room, which was suffused with the yellow light.

I felt as if the constantly closed windows were begging me to release them from their curse. In the corner of the room was an earthen water pot. In another corner was an earthen bowl filled with soil.

Since she was not allowed to go outside in daylight, she was to relieve herself in this bowl if necessary.

She must endure the stench until it got dark in the evening. At night, she would go out to leave the soil in the yard and fill the bowl again. The hard and testing plights of widowhood.

There was a glass tile on the roof. She deserved only the faint light that came in through it.

She found relief in the air that came in through a small rectangular gap above the window. What sin had she committed to deny her the pleasures of free air and sunlight?

As I stood there stunned, she looked me in the eye and asked,

"I had told you then not to tell anyone. But you told everyone. I do not know what will happen now."

I could sense that she was very scared. I stood just an arm's length away from her, wanting to hug and comfort her. I bent down and grabbed her arm. I held her tightly, although she tried to pull her hand away dismissively.

"Maka... Don't be afraid. Nothing will happen, Be brave."

I am not sure whether my words brought reprieve. But she looked at me with love as I called her by name. After her husband's death, she changed her name to Pappathi. The despair of giving up even one's name. I held her arm tight. My touch gave her the consolation that countless words cannot give. Tears welled in her eyes. The teardrops that slid down from her eyes shone like crystal balls, in the scant light glimmering from the kerosene lamp.

I had come out of the room resolutely. I had made a certain decision.

The postmaster's wife put the lamp out and locked the room as she came out. Darkness filled her room, without a grain of light left. Just like her life.

Her life should be filled with light. She should also be able to play freely, just like Thankamani and me. She also must get her due opportunities to be happy. I came down to the front yard.

In two corners, my father and the postmaster sat as if they had lost their ability to speak. At times, human beings are like that. Words are not enough for communication. The words sprouting within would die there.

"Let us go," Achen asked me as soon as he saw me coming out. I nodded in agreement. The postmaster's eyes met mine, asking me something. Despair filled his glance. The appeal is not to tell anything to anyone.

"Let Maka come and play with us, just like us. What is the problem?"

My father and the postmaster exchanged glances as my words pushed the odd silence away. They felt it was the meaningless blabber of an unintelligible child and gave a tired smile. I continued seriously as I understood them.

"This is not Mayiladuthurai. This is Sinthamanipudur. No one here knows anything about Maka. Let her come out and interact with all of us, just like us."

Although he listened to me, the postmaster remained impassive, as if he had nothing to hope for.

But I saw a glimmer of hope on my father's face.

With renewed energy, my father held the postmaster's hands together and said,

"Uma said it right. No one in this village knows anything about her. Let her come out freely and peacefully. If anyone asks you, say that your sister has just come from your village. Tell them that she shaved her head in a temple for penance. She is a young girl. Do not make her unhappy anymore. Let her be happy."

The postmaster also saw this as an opportunity to pull his sister out of the deep chasm into which she had fallen. Unable to control himself, he covered his face with his hands and wept. The tears flowed incessantly down his cheeks.

All his grief stemmed from the terrible fate of his sister trickled out.

Thus Pappathi, who should have lived a life equal to death with the heavy burden of widowhood, fluttered about in the sunshine of Sinthamanipudur.

How many women would have been able to emerge from the exiled life of widowhood with sindhur wiped from their foreheads, heads shaved and only a bare floor to lie down on to sleep?

But,

Maka's life was changing. Like a butterfly, she spread her wings and fluttered around.

TEN

Achamillai, achamillai, acham enbathu illaye,
Icckathulorellam yethirthu nindra podhilum,
Achamillai, achamillai, acham enbadhu illaye,

I am not afraid of anything.
There is no fear at all.
Even if the whole world is against me
I am not afraid of anything

While chanting this poem, I went on to fetch water. Thankamani began to tease me because she thought I was babbling pointlessly.

"What are you babbling about like you have gone crazy?"

She tapped me on the back with her pot. I became furious.

"You fool, this is a poem by the great poet Bharathiyaar.

"Do you know the meaning of *Achamillai, achamillai*?"

"Oh, go away, great Bharathiyaar poem!"

She pursed her lips and scoffed.

"I don't know."

She went on as if ignorance was not a sin. I put down my pot and stood, lifting my leg and placing it against the neck of the pot, arms outstretched as if I were MGR, chanting... as loud as I could.

"I am not afraid. I am not afraid.

Even if the whole world is against me,

I am not afraid."

Thankamani burst out laughing when she turned around and saw my posture. She was sitting in front of me like a spectator.

I looked at her and continued to sing earnestly. Every grain of sand and blade of grass on the road on which the morning sunlight fell were my spectators. I sang aloud.

"Thuchamagiyenni nammai thooru seidha podhilum,
Achamillai, achamillai, acham enbadhu illaye,

Even if someone thinks badly of me and annoys me, I am not afraid of anything.

Pichai vangi unnum vazhkkai petru vitta podhilum,
Achamillai, achamillai, acham enbadhu illaye,

Even though I have to beg for a living, I am not afraid of anything.

Ichai konda porulellam izhandhu vitta podhilum,
Achamillai, achamillai, acham enbadhu illaye.

Even if I lose everything I want, I am not afraid of anything.

My voice ended in that narrow alley.

I wanted to shout to stun all of Sinthamanipudur, but my voice was not strong enough for that. Still, I sang.

Achamillai, achamillai, acham enbathu illaye,

I felt that the words of Bharathiyaar also kindled a flame in Thankamani. But shouldn't women be humble and submissive? Her mother had taught her that.

That was her doubt too.

"No one can challenge society. Whatever it is, we have to be submissive to society."

How dare Thankamani, who grew up thinking that modesty is a virtue for women, rebel against society?

How many women can do it? She asked.

"Not many can be like Kannamakka."

Kannamakka was a brave woman from Sinthamanipudur. She wore a dhoti and a shirt like a man, and she looked like one too.

She always kept a lit cigarette on her lips. Dark complexion.

As tall as a man.

Sometimes she hung her dhoti high. Arms and legs with tight muscles. And a firm disposition.

I was five years old when I first saw her. When we were playing hide and seek, a truck came and stopped near us.

In those days, any vehicle aroused our curiosity. We hooted and ran toward it. Some tried to climb in and pull themselves up by the tires.

Some ran around the vehicle screaming.

I stayed away from the noise and watched everything.

I was stunned when I saw a rogue figure in the truck.

It was Kannamakka who came out with her dhoti raised.

After her, the driver also climbed down. He touchingly begged her for something.

"It's not going to be enough. Just give me more. Today's work was pretty tedious."

Kannamakka burned him with a look.

"You go... it's enough, that's all."

Mercilessly, she waved him off and searched for a beedi hidden in her shirt sleeve.

When she didn't find it, she looked around in disappointment.

With a wave of her hand, she beckoned me near her.

I walked towards her. She tossed a coin into my hand.

"Hi, girl, go to the shop and get me a bundle of beedi."

I held the coin and ran to the shop, bought the beedi and hurried back. She took the packet from me and rolled it in her palm like a cube. She took a beedi from it, lit it and took a puff. When she turned around, the driver was right behind her. She offered him a beedi and asked,

"Hey, why are you waiting? Do you need beedi? Here, take one and get rid of yourself."

He contorted his face in disappointment, waiting for her to do him a favor. Still, he looked at her and scratched his head. Kannamakka looked at him grimly. She stepped close to him and drew in another breath.

"Don't you want to go? This amount is enough for the work you have done. Take it and go. Don't stand in front of me."

"You bastard, don't you want to go?"

As Kannamakka spouted her expletives, he muttered something and left. It was as if he wanted to take revenge on the truck. He was driving too fast.

I heard that Kannamakka's main occupation was to clandestinely sell rice and provide girls to truck drivers. She illegally brought rice from Palakkad and sold it in Tamil Nadu. She ventured into the illegal rice trade in the 1960s when rice was scarce due to famine.

When both her parents died, her siblings also separated. She scraped by with odd jobs and survived. No one liked her because she listened to no one and allowed no one to control her. Secretly, some said that she was a curse for Sinthamanipudur.
Some even in public, if it would not reach her ears.

"Do not be afraid. Even if there is no one for you in this world, you can still live. Never be afraid of anything." She proved these words with her life.Thankamani asked for the same Kannamakka.

The answer was the words she had spoken.

"Should not we live when we have no one in this world? We must live without being afraid of anything, even if the whole world is against us."

Bharathiyaar's poems helped to awaken a sense of independence in the women of those days. These lines brought a new light to me. I shared them with Thankamani and other friends.

It was the energy of these poems that helped us to say no to marriage.

But,

Who can predict what time has in store for us? Who writes our destiny?

Thankamani has kept the words of her youth and still lives as an old maid. What has become of me who had the feeling of freedom that sprouted while reciting Bharathiyaar poems?

How could I get married and break my promise to my friends?

PART 2
ADOLESCENCE
Roots Deep Into The Soil

ONE

As I step out of childhood, what do I treasure? Heavy responsibilities. The hurting spearheads of ridicule. The fears of loneliness, or a serene life where colourful dreams never fade?

In my teens, I progressed from Kathirinmel School to Vandipudur Government Girls High School. The balance of my life included mocking and sympathetic looks because of the life lessons my mother and *Memma* taught me. My goal was to escape the tragedy of such torturous experiences. This led me to Vandipudur. To avoid questions related to my mother, I wrote in the admission register that my mother had passed away.

The second phase of my life began with the picnic we had at Guruvayoor in class eleven after the midterm examination. The group that went to Guruvayoor consisted of twelve girls and three teachers. On Saturday morning, we reached Guruvayoor by a Tamil Nadu Public Transport bus. We took a room at the Spill Green Lodge near the temple. We visited the temple and paid our respects.

As we talked in Tamil, people watched us. I was the only one in the group who could speak Malayalam. I still remembered the lessons my grandfather gave me.

Until noon, we spent our time in the temple itself. We also partook of the ritual lunch provided at the temple and returned to the lodge.

As we entered, someone at the reception called out to us,

"Hey, girl, wait."

I turned and looked at him. From the look on his face, I could tell he meant me. I got Thankamani and Hemalatha to stay as well. He approached us and asked with a smile.

"Aren't you Malayalees?"

"We are from Coimbatore," I replied.

He looked at each of us without taking his eyes off my face, he said, "Here I have seen a woman who looks just like you."

Not understanding his words, Hema and Thankamani approached me and asked in my ear what he had said.

I translated his words.

"He says he has seen someone whose face looks exactly like mine. She resembles me, it seems."

Astonished, the two looked at him. His face brightened.

"That's right, she's just like you. That's why I asked."

"No, we are all Tamil." Giggling, I walked towards them, flanked by Thankamani and Hema.

"Who is it? Shall we meet her?" asked Thankamani, unable to suppress her curiosity.

"Oh, no. It is said that there are seven persons in this world who are alike. Is it possible to meet each of them?"

Hema unravelled her wisdom.

Not only Thankamani, I too became curious. The desire to meet someone who looked like me grew within me.

I enquired from the receptionist for more details. He said he didn't know any details, but this was the woman he saw walking past the lodge every day.

Since he said he sees her between 8 and 8.30 am, we decided to meet her somehow the next morning. Our bus back to Coimbatore would leave at 7.30. If we missed it, the next bus would not come for two and a half hours. The teachers had insisted that we should all be ready by the time the bus left at 7.30 am. But if we left on that bus, how were we going to get the things done that we had planned? So, we were deliberately late.

We made Thankamani fake stomach ache. Though we might get scolded by the teachers, we were comforted by the fact that our plan would work. At 7:45 am, we stood in front of the lodge. We fixed our eyes in the direction the receptionist said she would come.

Time crept on slowly. Anxiously, we eyed each woman who approached from a distance. If they approached, it was not the person we were looking for.

The receptionist helped us along without disturbing his work at the desk. A large number of women walked past us. But none of them bore any resemblance to me.

Disappointed, we looked at him. He stood there helplessly.

"It's already past her normal time to come by. She usually comes at this time. Casting a glance into the distance, he muttered.

"What happened today?"

Disappointed, we returned. It was Thankamani's idea to write a letter and entrust it to him.

"I am writing this because I am very interested in seeing a person who looks like me. Please send me your photograph.

With love, Umadevi."

That was the content of the letter.

Hema's face showed how embarrassed she was to be unnecessarily scolded by the teachers. Thankamani and I were disappointed because our plan failed.

Even after returning to Sinthamanipudur, the same thoughts ran through Thankamani's mind.

"Will she send a photo when she sees the letter? I would like to meet the person who looks just like you." She seemed even more excited to meet this woman.

Although this thought kept coming up in our conversations over the next few days, we slowly forgot about it.

One afternoon a fortnight later.

I had dozed off in biology class and jumped up when the teacher called my name.

"Uma,"

All eyes turned to me. I stood up. I understood that she was reading my name from the slip of paper the attendant brought.

"The headmaster has called you."

As the teacher said this with a meaningful look, many thoughts ran through my mind. Why did he call me? I walked briskly to the headmaster's room. Although I have heard that he has a temper, I have never fallen prey to his wrath. I did nothing wrong that would have required his summons to the office. What would have happened then?

In the room sat not only the headmaster but also Gandhaamani teacher and Mallika teacher.

Mallika teacher was our class teacher. Gandhaamani teacher taught us the language.

Deep silence enveloped the room. Their faces were puffed up like balloons. The headmaster stared deeply at me, like a policeman at a thief. I felt slightly frightened. He pushed his glasses up and asked his first question.

"Uma, what did you tell us about your mother? What happened to her?"

A shiver ran through my body. Stunned, I looked at the teacher. When I saw him staring at me, my mouth went dry. I began to search for words.

The headmaster repeated his question in a sterner tone. I looked pityingly at the teachers who were staring at me.

When they looked at me without any sympathy, I hung my head. My silence further triggered his anger.

"Why would a girl lie at school that her mother is dead while she herself is still alive? What kind of impudence is that?"

Now things became clearer to me. The headmaster has exposed my lie that my mother has passed away. He thinks

I did it out of arrogance.

I wanted to say that I wrote it because I was afraid of being humiliated. My mouth frozen in fear would not let my tongue come to life.

"Uma, " The headmaster raised his voice and called me again. He held out a yellow postcard to me and said,

"Here, this letter is for you. Open it and read it."

With trembling hands, I took the card from him. A few words, neatly written in black ink. I felt as if they were smiling at me.

"Can't you read Malayalam? Read."

Mallika teacher, who had been silent till then, opened her mouth.

I stood there staring at the letter. Gandhaamani teacher came to rescue me as if she understood my plight.

"Read. Let me help you where you cannot."

She is the only one of them who knows Malayalam.

I held the postcard right in front of my face and read slowly as I put the letters together.

Dear Umakutty,

I have been waiting for you for so long! Amma is very sad to miss you and Thambikuttan."

As I read these two lines, I felt uneasy. Amma... Amma. I felt more angry than sad as I repeated that word in each line. I lifted my face from the card and looked at the headmaster. His posture reminded me of an animal ready to pounce on its prey. I looked at the postcard again. Why had she sent me this letter? When I was at a loss for words in between, Gandhaamani teacher came to my rescue. She took the letter from my hand and started from the place where I had stopped.

"I know you are angry with me for leaving you. You do not know your father's character. He behaved very badly towards me. You are too young to understand that. But God has given me this opportunity.

Amma will come to meet you. To take you with me.
With love
Amma

Gandhaamani teacher stopped reading and looked at me.

I stared at the floor to avoid their glances at me.

This did not make me sad. Instead, it only made me angrier.

The one who left the children and went in search of her pleasure says she loves..... and will visit us. I do not want to see anyone. Anger welled up inside me. I controlled myself. I did not feel like saying anything to anyone. Let the headmaster and the teachers blame me. What have I done wrong?

Is it mendacious if I said my mother is no longer there? Is it my fault that I did not know she was alive?

While these questions are running through my mind, the headmaster was preparing to go into a fit of rage.

"We cannot tolerate such an arrogant girl in our school anymore. I intend to give you a transfer certificate."

The news that they'd give me transfer certificate and send me away didn't move me. My insensitivity made him even angrier.

"We thought you were a diligent girl and now you have started lying and gone astray."

Gandhaamani teacher must have thought that I was in more danger from my silence, so she stepped closer to me and pleaded with the headmaster.

"Sir, forgive her and let it go this time. Let's make sure she doesn't do the same thing again."

Mallika teacher also spoke up for me.

Finally, the headmaster decided to let me go scot-free. Gandhaamani teacher scared me with her big eyes, warned me not to repeat similar mistakes in the future and handed me the letter.

With the letter in my hand, I walked out without a word.

I'd have loved to tear the yellow card into pieces and throw it into the cow-dung pit.

The black letters stood tall and mocked me, I felt.

Later, as I sat in class holding the letter in my hand, an important question came to mind.

"How did this letter get into the school now?"

I looked at the seal of the post office on the letter. It had been posted from Guruvayoor.

Now everything became clear to me. The woman that the lodge-keeper mentioned, who looked very much like me, was my mother. The anxiously written letter was addressed to her. When she read my name in the letter and the details mentioned by the receptionist at the lodge, she recognized me. I read the letter again. My eyes lingered on the last lines.

"Amma will come to see you. To take you back with me."

Love, Amma."

I didn't tear the letter into pieces. I didn't throw it off.

I stashed it in the leather suitcase where we kept our clothes.

I thought it would end there.

But, Time had something else in store.

I didn't tell anyone about my mother's letter. Thankamani kept asking me why the headmaster had summoned me, but I didn't tell her. I also hid it from my father.

Though it kept me in suspense for two or three days, I gradually forgot about the letter.

Two weeks passed.

It was a Monday. I didn't go to school that day because of a severe sore throat and fever. I had been plagued by tonsillitis since childhood. The same symptoms prevailed.

I went to the hospital with my father. The doctor advised us to remove the tonsils as I was chronically affected.

The doctors referred us to the ESI hospital in Coimbatore. I asked Thankamani to inform the school that I'd be absent for two or three days.

The ESI hospital in Coimbatore is very busy. People come from different places as the hospital offers almost all specialties and has many facilities. When we reached there, the hospital was full of people and vehicles. Although my fever had gone down, I still had an unbearable sore throat. When I saw the condition of some patients, my sore throat seemed very insignificant. There are many people around us who are suffering. These moments show us how helpless we are in the face of the disease.

The doctor instructed us to be admitted. He scheduled the operation for the next afternoon.

We had not expected this. Achen had not thought that we would have to stay another day.

As soon as we were admitted, we decided to go ahead with the operation. But there were no extra clothes to wear. When Achen said he would go and get our clothes and come back, I agreed. I was alone in the third bed in the general ward. The long corridor has almost ten beds.

Each bed was occupied by children and adults, patients and their attendants...

The pungent smell of medicines assailed my nose. The sore throat took on unbearable proportions. Like a needle boring into it.

I looked around.

Not a smiling face was to be seen.

They all looked indifferent.

I had the feeling that hospital beds were like burning places that robbed you of your courage. As I lay there like that, I fell asleep.

I do not know how long I slept. I opened my eyes and heard a loud scream. Stunned, everyone in the room looked outside. The scream came from there.

It came from the relatives of a scooter rider who had just died. He had been injured in an accident that morning.

I got up and looked through the window. Two women were beating their chests and shouting. One is an old woman and the other is young.

Is the other his wife?

I thought of Maka in vain.

Death is so horrible!

In the melee, I did not notice the middle-aged woman standing next to me.

The screams and crying died away.

My eyes met hers as the others retreated to their beds murmuring sympathetically.

A well-dressed lady in a purple saree.

"Amma, "

Whispered my lips involuntarily.

Seeing me looking at her with astonished eyes, she came and sat on my bed. The fragrance of her body invaded my nostrils.

She stroked my forehead with her fingers and called me lovingly.

" Uma,"

I kept my eyes closed and lay like that for a minute, enjoying the coolness of her fingers.

It was only for a fleeting moment.

I wished I could scream that I did not want to see her. But my tongue would not give in.

"Didn't you get the letter Amma sent?"

She asked in a hushed voice.

I lay there in silence.

"I went to your school. That's where I met... "

Her fingers kept stroking my forehead. I wanted to fight them off. But I could not.

I lay still.

No one becomes a mother just by giving birth. Motherhood only reaches its perfection when you take care of your children.

Can a woman who pushes children into unfathomable depths of misery be called a mother?

The disheartening smell of drugs and her intoxicating fragrance filled the room. All eyes were on the dolled-up woman. I looked at the exit door. I could not believe my eyes.

Leaning against the door, he stood there staring at us. Hot flames of anger blazed in his eyes, directed at no one in particular.

When she saw my father, she got up to leave. When she reached the door, she turned to him in a heavy voice.

"It is enough. All your caring and bringing up children. I will take them with me. If you resist, I will seek legal help. "

Achen's face turned red. It surprised me to see the change in my father's calm face, which was always brimming with love and affection. Though I kept thinking about it, I could not understand why my father did not respond to her challenge.

Achen did not ask me anything. Not just that day, until I came home after having my tonsils removed.

But the dark clouds on his face remained without rain.

I was relieved when they removed the ulcer that was plaguing my throat. But my father's change of mood worried me.

I inquired about the cause of his smouldering anger.

"What happened, Achaa?" I asked him, suppressing a sob.

"Is it because I met Amma at the hospital?"

He just stared at me angrily but said nothing.

I walked towards him and held his hand.

"Tell me why you are angry. Why are you angry with me? How am I responsible for her coming?" I rushed towards him and lost control.

"She did not come. Did not you bring her here?" I heard him shout and shuddered.

"Didn't you write a letter to get her? Go. She will take care of you. Achen is of bad character. That's why she left home, it seems. "

All his grief and anger burst forth like a raging river.

In my mind, I felt numb.

He had seen the letter I had hidden. He would have seen it when he opened the suitcase to take out my dress.

His tongue exhaled the words of the letter.

His anger at reading the letter would have doubled when he saw Amma in the hospital.

I felt bad.

Achen misunderstood me. He thinks I wrote the letter to invite her.

"Go, go away with her."

He kept talking non-stop.

"She will take care of them. They wrote a letter and called her because they felt Achen was not taking care of them. Go and be better."

A numb feeling grew throughout my body. I felt that the ulcer they had taken out of my throat had not left my body but was spreading everywhere, hurting me.

Unable even to cry, I stood motionless.

TWO

I had not expected such a climax. Although I did not long for new air or light, it was my fate.

Amma managed to uproot a plant firmly rooted in Sinthamanipudur and planted it in Guruvayoor. She sought legal help, just as she had challenged Achen at the hospital. He did not listen to my side of the story at all. Whenever I tried, he exploded. I was terrified to see him in a yet unknown way.

The people of Sinthamanipudur also blamed me. They sympathized with the fate of Compounder Balan. Both his wives had left him. Now his daughter too.

Only Thankamani understood me. She tried her best to convince her mother. She refused to listen to her.

She kept repeating her usual rhyme about women.

"A girl should be gentle and submissive. She had everything here. Why did she still decide to leave her father?"

She brought the sealed papers about her rights to her two children to take us to Guruvayoor. I held the hand of Thambikuttan, who was shocked, with the leather case and left the house. With each step forward, I looked back.

No, he did not come out to see us.

It was the daytime of the month of Aadi. The cloudy sky, ready to burst into tears, gloomy as my heart, stretched its umbrella over my head.

" Uma,"

Hearing someone calling me from behind, I turned and looked around.

It was Thankamani. She came running and hugged me. She kissed Thambikuttan several times on the cheeks. She held my hands together and whispered in my ear.

138

"Achamille... Achamille, don't be afraid, don't be afraid."

On my journey to Guruvayoor, I kept repeating this *Bharathiyaar* poem. I felt suffocated the moment I stepped out of the crowded row house in Sinthamanipudur into the luxurious three-bedroom house in Guruvayoor. I wanted to return somehow. Maybe I could change my father's misconceptions. I just wanted to live there.

"Let's go, Chechy. Let's go back to Achen."

Said Thambikuttan that night as he lay close beside me:

In my grief, I pressed my lips to his forehead. The darkness in that room frightened me.

The eternal darkness covered my eyes like a black curtain, hiding the bad omens of the future.

The next morning Amma told us many things. Words that were imbued with love.

But they were not enough to put our minds at ease. I looked at her with contempt. And at Palanichami with distaste, who always shadowed her.

I ignored this guy who wasn't even worth as much to us as a cheap songbook. In the days that followed, I felt like I was in a cage. We ate just enough to keep hunger at bay. Thambikuttan stayed with me like a tail.

We spent a week like this. Though Amma did her best to keep in touch, we drifted far apart like the parallel railway lines.

I needed only the air and sunlight of Sinthamanipudur. I closed all the windows tightly to avoid the new breeze and sunlight.

I don't want anything more. Amma is offering a life of fine fragrances. I don't want it. Temptations rose. I can continue my studies at any school in Thrissur. If I am interested, I can act in films. After living with her for a week, I understood that she had enough connections for that.

Theatre artists and filmmakers were guests there.

Although I tried to escape her, she caught up with me. To escape her, I refused to eat anything in protest. This worked.

"If she starves here, I will be in trouble. That's what's on her mind. Wrong upbringing. What else?"

Amma scolded.

"What's in you? Say it. We will do the same. "

Knowing I would not get a better opportunity, my reply was very quick.

"I want to study."

"I didn't say that you could not study."

"Not from here. I will not be able to study in this house. "

My rebellious voice annoyed her.

"If you plan to return to your goddamned father, I will not spare you or him."

The change in her choice of words over the week baffled me.

So, was she hiding so much deadly venom in her honeyed words all these days?

"I do not want to go to anyone. Leave me in some hostel or orphanage. I would say that I have no father or mother. "

Amma walked out in a rage.

My protest had won. She understood that I could not study anywhere in Kerala as I was learning in Tamil. After talking to a few people, she decided to enroll me in Sharada Mutt in Salem. She allowed me to stay in her hostel.

I felt sad when I thought of Thambikuttan. He could not join the Sharada Mutt. Besides, Amma was not very concerned about him. She did not offer him the same enticements as she did me. He was sent to a boarding school in Palakkad.

Apart from my feeling of missing him, life in Sharada Mutt was heavenly. Sharada Mutt School was run by Swaminis dressed in white and saffron.

The silver light of purity prevailed everywhere. There were strict instructions in the Mutt to keep the school and the hostel clean and pure. These instructions were also followed.

The new environment drove away the dark clouds from my sky.

New stars were rising there.

For the first two to three months, Amma paid the fees on time. Then she started paying in alternate months. Sometimes Amma came personally to pay the money. Sometimes other people were also there. She introduced them as film or theatre artists.

Amma worked as a Mahila Pradhan at the post office. This was the main source of income for her. Many entrusted their money to be deposited or paid at the post office.

I did not understand what Palanichami did for a living. Sometimes they fought over the money.

One of those days I got a letter from school. It said, 'Get good grades'.

At the bottom was a line, 'Love, Balakrishnan'. I was happy. The thought of my father enquiring about me made my eyes moist.

The happiness brought by the letter ended with a phone call the next day.

"Your mother is not well. Uma may go home." That's what the headmaster who took the call told me.

I wanted to tell him that I was not interested. But I did not say that. I did not want them to know about my problems.

I took the bus to Thrissur. What illness did she have that she had to be hospitalized?

And why should she even ask me to come?

A barrage of questions. Amma is a mountain of lies in human form. Will this be another outright lie?

As I got off the bus and walked home, an eagle circled high in the sky. Many mother hens would have hidden their chicks under their wings because they felt intimidated by the eagle. I reached the house where I lived for almost a week and felt suffocated. It was locked. I stood there not knowing what to do.

"Oh, have you come?" said the lady in the neighbouring house. I saw her once.

"Thankamani Chechy has moved away from here. Now she lives in Kottappadi. She called us and said you'd come."

"Here is the address." She went inside, picked up a piece of paper and handed it to me.

"It's very close by. You can take an autorickshaw and go there."

I nodded in agreement and went on foot to look for an autorickshaw.

The house in Kottappadi was smaller than the previous one. An old, unstylish house. I knocked and waited.

Just when I was in doubt, the big lie was in front of me.

How come Amma, who was in the hospital, was now at home? I was very upset but tried not to show it.

"What happened? You said you were at the hospital. "

"Oh, that......" She took me inside and told me in a light tone.

"I thought at least you'd come then." She sat down and pushed herself onto the red plastic chair in the hallway.

She looked at me pityingly.
"Come sit with me."

She pointed to another chair near her. I moved it and sat down with some distance.

"He cheated on me." When she looked me in the eyes as she said this, I wanted to laugh. Who would dare cheat on her? I looked at her questioningly.

"It was several lakh rupees that people had given me to deposit at the post office.

He took it away.

"Amma tried to tell me that Palanichami, who had lived with her for more than ten years, had cheated her, stolen money and run away. I didn't believe it.

"Amma is in a terrible mess. I've to give the money back.

I don't see any other way." There is no other way, that is, she has found a way. What way is that? I sat there wide-eyed. She moved her chair close to mine with a calm and gentle face.

"Amma has arranged everything. It's a new film. They have agreed to give you a part in it. It's the only solution I've now."

An ember of protest flared up in my chest. I felt like gouging out this shameless creature's eyes and burning her alive.

"So, are you looking for me because you want me to solve your problems?" I rose from the chair and asked her in a heavy voice.

She was slightly taken aback, but not shocked.

I guess it's my own fault for coming all the way here and believing your lie. So, I can be in movies."

My voice echoed within the four walls of the room like a sob.

She sat still even though I exploded. It made my anger cascade. I took the bag in my arm.

"I want to go back. I'll go back to my father. After that, you'll not meet me. "She stood up and held my hand to placate me. I brushed her hand away.

"Don't choose cinema if you don't like it. It's because Amma has no other option. I won't ask you to do the same again. You study. "

I didn't trust her words.

I took the bus back to Salem. An eagle still hovered in the sky.

THREE

At Kathirinmel School, Snehalatha teacher has told us that love can cure any sorrow while teaching us the life of Mother Teresa. I always had an irrepressible urge to meet this holy woman who filled the lives of countless people with love and compassion and participate in her charitable activities.

Later, I read more about Mother Teresa and her Missionaries of Charity, who cast the light of love on starving people in slums full of darkness, took in orphans and cared for the sick.

Since my life lost its rhythm, my desire to live with Mother Teresa has peaked. So, during my school days at Vandipudur Government School and Sharada Mutt School, I wrote incessantly to Mother Teresa. Though I never received a reply, I continued to write without losing hope. I firmly believed that the Mother who had compassion on the poor would not ignore me.

During the final examination in twelfth grade, I was very distracted. The thought of where I would go after the exams worried me. I could not even think of returning to my mother. Apart from my father, I have no one to rely on. While other students were worrying about the exam itself, the thought of the exam was burning in my mind.

Mother Teresa burned brightly in my mind shrouded in darkness. A candle that melts for others. How could she not see me?

Am I not an orphan like her?

Mother Teresa used to tell the people around her that she was walking all alone in the darkness. Am I not also walking on a dark path?

The darkness frightens me. I am all alone.

The day the second exam was over, the hostel father called me. My incessant prayers were answered.

"Uma, who do you have at the Missionaries of Charity in Calcutta?"

When the warden, who always looks cheerful, asked me more cheerfully, I replied effusively, "Mother Teresa."

She filled my thoughts.

The warden laughed out loud.

"Someone you know?"

I knew my answer would be Mother Teresa again. But I did not say it. I took the letter and ran to my room.

My heart pounded as I opened and read the letter. I jumped for joy as I finished reading the letter.

"Dear daughter,

Mother would like to meet you. Come to the missionary.

With prayers,

Sister Vinitha

Just two sentences. But they were enough for me. My meagre hopes have come true. Has the dark phase of my life evaporated by itself?

Will I see light again in my dark sky?

I waited eagerly for the exams to be over. My thoughts revolved only around Mother Teresa and the Missionaries of Charity.

On the day I finished the exams, I went to Sinthamanipudur by bus. I have to tell the details to my father. Now I have only my father to confide in.

It has been months since I enjoyed the air and sun of Sinthamanipudur. I have grown stronger in this sun.

First, I went to Thankamani's house. Thankamani came running and embraced me. Our eyes became moist.

"Uma, you have grown up a little."

With motherly affection she took my hand.

"Have you seen your father?"

Thankamani's mother asked as she inquired about my whereabouts. I shook my head in the negative.

"After you left, his condition deteriorated."

In a pathetic tone, she said, leaving me stunned.

"Let me come with you. Let us go to your house."

Thinking that my father was still angry with me, they escorted me to my house. I followed them with Thankamani. I was reluctant to tell them that he was not angry with me or that he had sent me a letter.

He was engrossed in a book he was reading in a deck chair in the front veranda. When I entered the house, I felt an indescribable sense of security. Was not this where my life unfolded its shoots? Everyone feels connected to the soil that raised them. I felt the same. Next to the womb of one's mother, the house where one was born and brought up is the safest.

" Balaa ..."

Thankamani's mother cried as she entered the house. My father lowered the book in his hand and looked in the direction from which the call came. He was dazed when he saw me. His lips murmured my name.

It looked as if Achen had grown older. His moustache and beard looked like they had been polished silver to make that clear.

He stood up and came towards me. No one spoke a word. The silence was broken only by the rhythm of our breathing.

I put my bag down on the floor. I hugged him tightly. When I put my head against his chest, it felt as red hot as burning coals.

"There is rice cooking in my kitchen, let me go."

Thankamani's mother planned to leave us alone for a while. She heaved a long sigh. When she was on her way to her house, she turned around once again and looked at us.

As Thankamani stood there stunned, her mother patted her on the head and took her along.

Although we had a lot to tell each other, there was an eloquent silence between us for quite a while. Finally, I broke the silence and explained why I had come.

"Achaa, I want to go to the Missionaries of Charity in Calcutta. I got a reply to the letter I wrote to them."

Achen tried to say something. But unable to find the words, he swallowed what he wanted to say. His tearless, dry eyes looked at me helplessly.

Should it have come to this? What happened in your life that you wanted to sacrifice for others? Why are you so indifferent in life?

My father would have had many questions in his mind. But the words that came out of her mouth were different.

"What has happened to your life with your mother?"

"I do not want to go back to her. You come with me to Calcutta. Take me to Mother."

I did not feel like telling him more.

It was Uma's decision. My father knows she will not change. Who else but my father knows the stubborn girl who could get her wishes fulfilled?

"But Uma..."

Achen kept reminding me of the pros and cons of my decision.

"These decisions are not as simple as you think. They affect your future. If you go anywhere without your mother's permission, it will only make the problems worse."

It was obvious that Achen was afraid of her. He knew very well that she, who had gained the right over me, was capable of anything. Out of this fear, he tried to discourage me. But I stood by my decision.

"If you do not come, I will go alone."

My firm voice frightened him. My father stood in front of me and hung his head. My father could not help worrying about my future.

His daughter is brave. She is ready to face all odds. He understood that very well and that may have made him agree to my decision.

It was in March, at a noon that we started our journey to Calcutta. My heart was pounding as I drove from the narrow lanes of Sinthamanipudur to the Bengal heartland with its ancient palaces testifying to the glory of the British era. As we travelled some distance, we saw the narrow streets. Dilapidated buildings, streets with shady trees on either side, people pulling rickshaws with bare feet, the headlong workers...

We reached Nirmal Hridaya on Kali Street. The place where they shelter the people who would otherwise die like animals on the street. When we got there, ambulances kept arriving with patients sent away from hospitals. It is a dilapidated temple. It was the very first nursing home Mother Teresa established in Calcutta for the poor and homeless.

As we entered, we saw the white-clad nuns absorbed in their work. Suddenly a fear rose in me. I set out, throwing away my worries, ready to serve. But what am I to do here? What will mother ask when she meets me?

I looked at my father. The man who had taught the great lessons of service looked unsettled by what he saw around him. Did he feel disturbed because he thought the scenes around him were even more frightening than what he had seen? There are so many poor and helpless people around us.

As we stood there dazed, an angel dressed in white approached us and asked us our details. She smiled at us while we were unable to say a word and repeated her questions. First in Hindi and then in English.

Not wanting to waste time talking, I gave her the letter I had. She ran her eyes over the words of the letter, which was crumpled and sweaty.

"Sister Vinitha, Ok. You want to meet her. Come."

She invited us into the inner room. We followed her steps.

"Please sit here."

She pointed to the blue sofa in the corner of the room and said to us.

"I will call her."

We sat down on the sofa. Achen was still like a child, marvelling at the scenes around him. My eyes looked around the room. They lingered on a large picture hanging on a nail on the white wall. A hand holding a tiny outstretched finger.

My memories wandered back to Vandipudur Government

Girls School. Snehalatha teacher's lessons about Mother.

"In 1910, at the age of eighteen, Mother Teresa came to India of her own accord with the Macedonian Loretto Sisters."

"She organized a spiritual group called Missionaries of Charity to care for the poor and sick. When she left the Lady Loretto Sisters on 17 August 1948, she was wearing a white saree with a blue border and had only five rupees with her."

"She left the formal dress of the Loretto sisters and adopted the white cotton saree with the blue trim when she saw the Calcutta Municipal Corporation cleaners. They wore similar dresses. Mother would have thought there was no better dress than this to live among and serve the poor."

I am now going to meet Mother Teresa, who has answered God's call to work among the starving poor, in person. I was very excited.

"Uma..."

When I heard someone call my name, I stood up with folded hands.

From the letter I had given her, she knew I was Uma. Sister Vinitha was very young. A graceful and friendly face.

"Mother is in prayer." Touching my folded hands, she said.

She looked at my father, who was huddled beside the sofa, bowing. He too stood with folded hands.

After asking us to take our seats, the nun sat down on a chair opposite us. The grace in her manner and words attracted me.

She inquired from him about the details of our family. During the conversation, my father mentioned that I was a motherless child. She did not ask about the details.

The sister chatted with us for almost five minutes. It was only about the Missionary's activities and the patients.

In between, she interrupted the conversation. The nun stood up.

"Let me check whether Mother has finished her prayers or not."

The sister asked our permission and went in. When my father saw the gleam in my eyes, he smiled at me. I think his conversation with the sister had wiped away his misgivings.

"Uma...come..."

Hearing the nun calling me, I stood up. Taking the cue, she asked my hesitant father to come too.

We went into the inner room. Sunlight streamed through the open windows into the tidy and beautiful room. In the corner of the room stood a table and a chair. On the table were neatly arranged books.

On the neatly whitewashed wall hung a large painting of Christ. As I stood there in amazement, the face appeared behind the blue curtain, shining with the light of a thousand suns.

Here is the physical figure that gives light to the world

before me. From the lips of unceasing prayer came to me a flower-like smile.

Mother Teresa, who consecrated herself as the bride of Jesus Christ at the age of eighteen, has brightened so many lives! It took me some time to recover from the surprising encounter with the person I was constantly worshipping in my mind. As soon as I came back to reality, I bent down to touch her feet. Mother held me by both shoulders and lifted me up. She put her hand on my head and blessed me. Her touch spread through my body like a bolt of electricity.

"Uma has come to do service," Sister Vinitha said.

Hearing this, a tender voice came from the smiling lips of the Mother.

"Uma, love begins at home. We can take that love to our neighbour, to the street where we live, and then to the whole world. "

Your earnestness is good. But to do service you need not travel so far. Uma... Look around you. There are so many waiting for a little smile or a gentle touch. Can you pretend not to see them and walk here?"

Her words flooded into my heart.

I stood there listening to her words breathlessly. Or I didn't know what to say to her. A figure I longed to see. A voice I longed to hear. Her radiance made my body feel light. My spirit had become light as a feather.

Then Mother spoke to my father, who stood stunned.

"Let Uma study. Let's decide when she finishes her studies. These doors will always be open for her."

His face paled. He stood there as if something was troubling him. A man steeled and matured by life can do nothing but worry about his daughter.

Mother put her hand on my head again and blessed me. She looked into my eyes and smiled. The eyes spoke a language deeper than words.

We walked outside in silence.

When we reached the door, my eyes turned back to her.

Mother stood there, still smiling. I felt those two eyes speaking to me. The beads of her rosary flowed obediently between her fingers, giving comfort to thousands of poor people.

FOUR

As the sun grew colder, we returned to Sinthamanipudur. The question 'What next' kept on occupying my mind. The enthusiasm with which I had gone to Calcutta fizzled out. The dream that I would be able to join the activities of Mother and Missionaries of Charity was shattered. But I felt very happy that I could meet Mother Teresa and was blessed by her. My father's heart was also overjoyed on that occasion.

But is it likely that these things happened in this way?

"What Mother said is right. Now it is time for your studies, Uma." While we were returning, my father patted me on the back and said,

I could only sit silently and look at him. I have to study. But at whose mercy? Father or mother?

He read my mind through my eyes.

"Let us get a degree. I will teach you. But first go and convince her."

Is he submitting to my mother, who has asserted her right to her daughter, or is it his fear of a woman who doesn't mind going to extremes? I felt like asking him what emotion made him talk like that.

A light breeze, carrying the heat of the midday sun, brushed my hair and passed. That question too passed, along with many others I never asked.

A father's heart worries about his daughter's future. The bitter experience has made him such a coward that he is unable to make a firm decision.

I never wanted to go back to my mother. But I am not able to fly like a balloon filled with air. My mind was filled with the knowledge that there was a string attached to the balloon, and that string was in the hands of my mother, who had asserted her rights over me because of the biological connection through the umbilical cord. Either I have to inflate myself, or...

The second case occurred.

When I returned to my father, I had made up my mind. I must continue my studies. Then I will look for a job. I must live without seeking support from others. I must continue to practice the great lessons of compassion as my life's mission. Mother Teresa and the Missionaries of Charity were still on my mind.

When I went to my mother's house in Kottappadi, it was raining continuously. The rain cooled the earth and the spirit. After knocking on the door, I turned around and looked into the slanting rain. It was Amma's *Ilayamma* who opened the door. It had been so long since I had seen *Ammamma* (grandmother). Her face looked older than her actual age.

"Oh, you have come," she said, opening the door and inviting me in.

"Thankamani said you would come this week." I couldn't figure out how she knew that, as much as I thought about it.

"When did *Ammamma* come?"

Smiling, I inquired of her.

"It's been two weeks. I would have been living there, huddled in a corner somewhere. She made me come and said there was no one there for her." *Ammamma* said this with a plaintive tone.

Since I could not see Amma anywhere, I asked her in a low voice.

"Where is she?" Did *Ammamma* understand that I was even hesitant to call her Amma?

"Oh, what can I say? Now she's into drama. They are rehearsing in a nearby hotel. She is running after it, day and night."

In a plaintive tone, she mentioned something else. It is the rehearsal for a drama directed by Kalathil Ravi. There are many actors and filmmakers involved. Amma also plays a role in the drama.

The next morning, she came home. When she saw me, she expressed her affection for me unusually clearly. I had the feeling that she was repeating her play in real life too. It crushed me.

"I have to keep studying."

As we sat down to lunch, I expressed my need. I let her know that this was my goal. I told her about it so that she would not make evil plans about me in the joy of seeing me.

"Why not? Let us wait for the results and then go to university." She said it in a soft voice. A demeanour marked by love and affection. I was confused and could not understand what was going on. Did she decide to correct her mistakes?

In the evening she had gone to rehearsal. Later, some people came home and asked about her. *Ammamma* spoke to them. Their words and looks were rude. Though I was scared, *Ammamma*'s presence made me feel safe.

"Oh, this has been going on for a while now. Some people come and argue. "

As they left and locked the door, she said,

"They are talking about money. That it has not been sent to the post office or has not arrived and so on. I do not know. My god, Krishna."

Her lips, dry with fear, were filled with piety. I sat there relieved that these problems would not affect me.

The next day Amma did not come home. In the evening, an auto rickshaw came and stopped in front of our house. The driver got out and knocked on our door.

"Thankamani Chechy sent me..." he said as *Ammamma* opened the door.

"To take you..." he finished his words.

"Where to?"

"To the rehearsal camp."

He looked *Ammamma* in the eye, who looked doubtful, and said, "Chechy said you would be ready now. "

Ammamma looked at me helplessly. I shrugged my shoulders to express my displeasure. He is still waiting. How should I express my feelings and thoughts to him?

"Today is the dress rehearsal. Sunday is the first performance."

He was still talking about the drama. All this time I was thinking about how to solve the problems in my life. Although I doubted my mother's unusual behaviour, I did not think she would set another trap for me. "

"What did you decide?" *Ammama*'s voice was tired. I raised my head and looked at her. She had an unhappy expression on her face.

"If we do not go, that will blow her up...... Sometimes she does not even consider I am her mother. "

Ammamma tried to placate herself with her frank talk.

Did not Achen have the same fears? Otherwise I would not have had to come here again. Even my heart was ready to forget everything and forgive.

But it seemed unstoppable.

When we reached the rehearsal camp, it was moderately crowded with people. Some of them I had also seen with Amma. Amma introduced me to some of them. I went with her without letting known that my spirit was angry.

Some crossed the line.

"Chechy, your daughter will shine in the theatre."

A bearded man was watching me down to his toes, blowing up the smoke from his cigarette.

"She's not aiming for drama, by the way, she's aiming for cinema," the man sitting next to him said with a sly grin. I stood there silently, like a fool.

Yet they continued to make jokes about me, like passing

the parcel. Amma was not worried about this hurting my self-esteem.

Ammamma waited for us inert in a corner, away from people's gaze. I thought old age was holding an umbrella of safety over her head.

Otherwise, she too would have stood there tense, exposed to the stares and mischievous remarks of the crowd.

I felt that the men saw the female body like the dark blue butterfly-pea flower that used to grow in the courtyards of Sinthamanipudur. When the flower blooms, it resembles a beautiful butterfly and every eye delights in it. When life is over, it will fold and wither; it will fall to the earth. No one would pay any more attention to it. No foot would think twice before trampling it.

While enduring the pain and insult, I came out and held *Ammamma*'s hand. The feeling of loneliness turned me upside down. Restless thoughts gathered in my head.

In the crowd, a handsome, bearded face stared at me. With a gleeful laugh, he looked at my pale face through the rising smoke of the cigarette on his lips. Later, that face was to change my life forever. Why did I have to shrink my orbit for him?

FIVE

I could not sleep. Thoughts kept surfacing that made my mind restless. I tossed and turned in bed trying to sleep. There was just no sleep. Like a yacht caught in the waves of a stormy ocean, my thoughts rolled on.

My life is not a drama or a cinema. I cannot find happiness in it. I do not desire such a life.

The next day I visited Gracy Aunty, our neighbour. I was introduced to her on my last visit. She speaks with a broad smile. Her words, full of love and compassion, drew me in. She is almost forty. She has two sons. Her husband, Jose uncle, works in Kuwait. I opened the gate and went inside. They have various plants in the yard. She was watering the plants when I entered.

She came towards me joyfully as soon as she saw me.

"Come, dear... Come in." With her usual smile, she invited me in.

I followed her into the house. The hall is very nicely decorated. There is a large picture of Mother Mary on the wall. There are some trophies and medals on display. Her two sons are good at learning. Gracy Aunty also told me about her love for music.

"Do you want me to bring you some idlies?"

Gracy Aunty would like to please me.

"No, aunty. I have already eaten... " I lied. I was not hungry. It was not my stomach that needed food. I needed food and medicine to heal the burning in my troubled heart.

"Let me make some tea." She is not in the mood to let me go. "Do not think of leaving without eating something. Please sit here. I will bring you some tea."

As she went into the kitchen, I followed her.

"Let me come with you."

A tidy kitchen. It looked like she did not compromise on hygiene. You could feel that as soon as you entered the house. The house looked as clean as her heart.

"Aunty..."

Without lifting her head, she answered my call while adding tea dust to the boiling milk.

"Yes, dear?"

"Aunty, the last time we met, you told me about a church. One that looks after orphans?"

"Oh yes, St Lawrence Church, is not it?"

She asked me as she turned off the cooking gas and took the tea off the stove. I just looked at her, because I did not remember.

"But it's not St Lawrence Church that looks after the children. It's the Pope Hall Peace Home run by Bishop Joseph Kundukulam."

She poured the tea into the white cup emblazoned with a red heart, handed it to me and asked.

"Why, dear? Why did you ask about the church?"

I was perplexed as to how to answer her. What relationship do I have with her to tell her my burning inner turmoil? Words failed me in my mouth. I looked at her and sipped the lukewarm tea. She waited. Tensely listening to what I was going to say to her.

Should I talk about my insecure life? Or about the possibilities of saving myself. I began to sweat profusely under the rapidly spinning ceiling fan. Finally, the words split, opened my mouth and gushed out.

"I want to go to the Pope Hall Peace Home. "

I waited for her reply. Her smile had disappeared.

She came and sat close to me, lifted my face and asked.

"Why, dear? What happened to you?"

Her tone carried a motherly affection. Her face, which

always carried a smile, looked grave. I broke into sobs. She placed her hand on my shoulder to pacify me.

Controlling my tears, I told her everything. My childhood without joy, my adolescence without any desire, the days that I passed holding my sorrows back...

She listened to me hold her breath as I described the events until I met Mother Teresa, eager to do community service. She was breathless, unable to utter a word, and trying to hold her emotions.

Again, I said it in a pleading voice.

"Aunty, please take me to the bishop. I cannot continue like this. "

I thought all my sorrows held up in my heart would burst into tears. Though pitiable, I kept my control.

She sat quietly for a little while. The sorrow shading her eyes didn't suit her face.

"I knew something was going on at that house. From the day they came to live here... "

She halted what she was about to say, losing her courage to say it on my face.

" Let me introduce you to the priest at St. Lawrence Church. He will help you reach the bishop. "

My moist eyes cleared. A faint light spread. I got up to bid her goodbye.

While I was stepping out, she followed me and called me.

"Dear., "

" Don't let her know about this. Or else, she will not let me live here in peace. "

Hearing her words, I felt like laughing. Who is she to scare everyone? Is my mother a riddle that no one understands?

The same day evening, Gracy Aunty took me to St. Lawrence Church and told the details to the priest. The next day, I went to the Pope John Paul Peace Home at Ambalapuram Peringaandoor.

I told everything to *Ammamma* before leaving. Her aged heart grieved hearing everything. When she understood that I was firm in my decision, she placed her hand on my head, blessed me, and said, "May good things come to you. You manage yourself. There is no one else yearning for your well-being."

A sense of weariness was evident in the words of that elderly woman, who had lost her peace in her last days.

"I am leaving too. I have had enough. Let her do what she wants."

Do I have enough sympathy left in me to show her? I am more tired of this place than her.

The sky had grown dark when I reached Pope John Paul Peace Home. Even my mind had a cloud, eager to pour out everything pent up inside.

When I reached Pope John Paul Home, a slight drizzle had begun. Raindrops were falling along the wide courtyard. I ran, entered the portico, and waited there. The Peace Home stood there as if it were wearing a white saree with a blue border. It was a big, two-story building.

When Pope John Paul II visited India, he met the Thrissur Archbishop, and at that time, this Peace Home was named after him. The organization was inaugurated on February 7, 1986. Starting a home for the homeless like this was a dream for Kundukulam Achen.

I went inside. As I expressed my intention, a fair, slender nun took me to the bishop's room.

I bowed to the bishop as I saw him. He responded to my greeting. I gave him the letter from the priest of St. Lawrence Church. He took the letter and started reading. I kept observing him as he went on reading.

Bald with square spectacles. No moustache or beard. A chain with a cross stretched from his neck touched the belly.

A serious face, though a faint smile, remained on his lips. Bishop Joseph Kundukulam is known as the bishop for the poor.

"Umadevi,"

He pushed his glasses up his nose and called me.

"Now what is the reason for this wish?"

Since I had already anticipated this question, I was able to answer him without much thought.

"It is not now, Father. I have had this wish since childhood."

The bishop smiled mildly.

I told him about my childhood in Sinthamanipudur. I described how I used to visit the houses of Gounders and Chakliar Colony. I could not hold back as I told about my efforts to meet Mother Teresa and the opportunity that came my way. When I finished, I felt that I had used sincere words. The bishop was very touched by these words.

"It would not be difficult for you to join us. But this decision should not be taken on the basis of an emotional outburst. You will have to take care of people of different kinds. Some people suffer from incurable diseases, have mental problems or are lonely in old age." After a moment of silence, looking me in the eye, he continued.

"Service must not be done to resent someone or to get revenge. It must be done with devotion. The body and soul should be completely dedicated to it. "

I stood listening to the bishop's words with rapt attention. The words Mother had said rushed back into my mind. Those who are ready to serve will always see the helpless people before them. Yes, I see them. Right before my eyes I see them.

People who are chronically ill, mentally ill or with painful ulcers. There are so many helpless people.

"No, Father... My decision is not based on resentment or revenge. I have devoted my body and mind entirely to helpless people."

The bishop, as if understanding my firm decision, called me to him with a smile and showered me with his blessings. A chant of prayer sounded on his lips. Outside, it was raining heavily. A cold breeze blowing in through the window grill made a slanting raindrop trickle on my face. A faint chill spread through my body.

Even on the first day, I had the feeling that fate had reserved this home of peace for me. The bishop, who interacts with fatherly love, the sisters, who look at me like a sibling, and also the other inmates - I felt that we had to find our happiness ourselves. I found it. The Pope John Paul Peace Home became a happy home for me.

There were many people who were very old, ill or mentally ill. On the second day, I joined the sisters in my chosen area of activity. Some just have to get their medication. Others you even have to help them get out of bed. They have to be lifted out of bed, brushed and fed. Without any fatigue or inexperience, I brushed their teeth, washed them, cleaned their wounds, applied ointments and joined the others. The sisters were amazed at what I did. That day, at evening prayer, Sister Stella even mentioned it.

"Uma caught us off guard. This little girl started taking care of our patients like a person with several years of experience. I was surprised how she talks to them and laughs and does things for them as if she were one of them."

The other sisters clapped and congratulated me. I was proud. I wanted to tell them that I had got used to them. That's a good lesson my father taught me.

I remember the first day I visited the Gounders' house. The room smelled of someone's festering sores. An old woman is screaming because she cannot bear the pain of the leg with the festering sores. My father is sitting next to her, cleaning and dressing the wounds. I hid in the corner of the room, full of horror and fear...

"Uma, when you grow up, you will be able to see her as your grandmother." My father's words echoed in my heart.

I wanted to stand up and measure my height. Have I grown tall? Today I took care of them as if every one of them belonged to me. So, I must have grown taller...

Amma was waiting to finish her preoccupation with the drama. She had known that I had gone to Peace Home. In her tantrum, she quarrelled with *Ammamma* and Gracy Aunty. Unable to bear her remorse, *Ammamma* went back to her house.

Was she going to keep me as a prisoner? Did she decide that she would not let me enjoy happiness and peace?

The day after the first performance of the drama, she came to meet the bishop. The bishop also sent for me.

"Father, please do not think that I am a heartless mother. I want my daughter to aim high. "

I felt that she was reciting a dialogue she had memorized for the play in front of the bishop. He sat quietly and listened to it all. She cried and recounted her experiences. She told crude lies, such as that her life was ruined by our father's misbehaviour and that he isolated her daughter from her.

I noticed a slight annoyance flash on the bishop's face. I had told him everything truthfully. But did he believe in this drama?

I tried hard not to betray my confusion, nervousness and anger.

"Let Uma decide." The bishop sounded firm. She came of her own accord. Peace Home will not turn away those who are willing to do their service. The bishop made his point by looking into my mother's eyes, which had a pitying expression. Amma frowned and looked at me.

I wanted to shout that Amma was talking pure nonsense. But those words did not come out. Only these words came out.

"I set out of my own free will. I have decided to continue here."

In her distaste, she turned her face away. To appease her, the bishop said,

"Let Uma stay here as she wishes. Let her also continue her studies. It is very rare to have such godly thoughts at such a young age. Only those who have a good heart are able to do so. Uma has it in her."

The fervour in the bishop's words excited me. I felt that his words were a great expression of appreciation for me. Amma hung her head for a moment, as if she had been defeated, and walked out.

The bishop, understanding the anger in her, advised me. "Uma, our kindness should not be extended only to strangers. How can a person who is unkind to his parents and siblings express this to others?

Do not hurt your mother."

Sadly, I lowered my face.

The next week passed uneventfully. I spent those days thinking of nothing else and devoted all my time, body and mind to service. But that day itself, as Amma left the Bishop's house defeated, she began to move the figures in her head. A week later, this culminated in her big show at the Bishop's house, with ten to fifteen people with her.

She misinformed the members of a Hindu association that this was a ploy to change her daughter's religion. She wanted to fight them collectively. I was saddened and frightened at the thought that the crowd in front of the Bishop's house was because of me. The bishop tried to settle the matter amicably by discussing it with the leadership of the association.

He invited them to the Peace Home and told them that there was no religious conversion there. Nevertheless, some of those who wanted to spout the poison of communal disharmony and destroy everything became indignant and started using swear words. Finally, he had to ask me to explain the facts to them because he had no other option.

I announced to them that I had come to the Peace Home of my own free will, that no one had converted me from my religion and that I was still Uma.

"I will tell everything in public. I will shout that you are trying to trample on my self-respect and my life. I will talk about everything you have done. "

My threat worked. Not wanting to lose face in front of the people she had brought with her, she waved it off.

But the bishop had to face pressure from his church. The church instructed him not to get involved in such emotional matters. But, my days at Peace Home brought new insights into life. The past and present of each resident helped me understand the helplessness of human life. My appreciation for being part of the peace at the Peace Home, which offers shelter to helpless people, grew.

But the dark phase of my life was not over yet. It was as if the woman who carried me in her womb for ten months had taken a vow to chase me out of any hole I could hide in.

It was at this time that her financial worries worsened. It had been almost a month and a half since I had reached the Peace Home. At noon, two people came to the bishop complaining about the money she owed them. They said that every time they asked her to repay the money, she excused herself by referring to her daughter. She lied to many that there was money deposited in her daughter's account and that it could only be released when she was eighteen years old. Every day she repeated similar lies. I understood that the bishop and the inmates of the Peace Home were losing their peace of mind because of me. One evening, the bishop called me to his office.

" Uma,"

His tone told me that what he had to discuss was very serious.

"You would have understood the situation here. It is a place where sick and old people live. We should not do anything to disturb their peaceful life."

I understood very well what the bishop was trying to say. Suddenly I felt a burning in my chest. My eyes became watery. I quickly wiped my face so that he could not see it.

"I understand Uma's situation. We have just resolved the earlier problems. If it happens again like this…."

He did not finish the sentence as if he understood my grief.

He lifted my face, which I had been holding down in grief and pain, and said,

"Today Uma's mother called again. She told about her problems. Financial problems. That's it. People are threatening her to pay back the money. Uma, just go home and check… "

I was forced to believe that time was merciless. I felt isolated. Where should I fly to? Into what high airs should I fly to free myself?

The bishop and the inmates of the Peace Home never doubted my abilities and my dedication. But they do not have the strength to bear the spearheads of accusations against me.

I should not be the reason to break the peace at Peace Home or for its inmates.

As I was saying goodbye, the bishop smiled and said to me.

"Uma, you can come back anytime you want. No one will be able to shake your resolve even if they try. "

I am caught in the rapids of time. I can no longer defend myself, but I continue to flow.

SIX

Amma looked unusually puzzled. Although I felt upset and annoyed at the situation, I sat there with an air of indifference. Although she had been through many difficult situations, the people who owed her money got organized.

They went from persuasion to threats. Many of them came home regularly and made trouble.

" Uma, "

She called me and touched my hand. This touch was loaded with many hidden meanings.

" I did not care for you. Yes, that is true. I know you are angry with me. But now please listen to me. " Her eyes looked at me pleadingly.

I had no doubt that she would tell me unbelievable lies. At any moment, my suppressed anger would burst and burst out of my chest.

It is no use. I must control myself. Although I have only lived at Peace Home for a short time, the lessons I have learnt will last me a lifetime.

This life is about forgiving and tolerating. This life is not about holding grudges or fighting each other.

"I do not want to drag you into my messed up life. But right now, I am not in control of things."

She looked at me helplessly. I continued my silence.

"It's not just one or two, but my debts amount to several lakhs of rupees. I have no idea how to pay them back. This has now come up with the police."

I said nothing. I did not think she expected an answer from me. She was just too eager to finish what she wanted to say.

" I have decided not to come here for the time being."

I lifted my face and looked at her doubtfully. I wanted to ask her why she would punish me for this.

She replied as if she understood me.

" If I am not here, they will come after you. They will harass you. They are without morals and without concern.

What they would say or do...." She broke off her words and held me by the shoulder.

This touch made me feel uncomfortable. I shrugged my shoulders, moved away a little and said it impassively.

" I will go to my father. Only you should not bother me."

I did not use a pleading tone. I could not shout while helplessness and a sense of defeat were reflected on her face. Instead, I expressed my protest in a calm tone.

Amma kept her gaze fixed in the distance and said,

" They also know Sinthamanipudur. If they do not see me, they will follow you there too. "

I was speechless, unable to say anything. I looked into her eyes, unable to decipher the truth and the lie in her words. I felt fear shadowing her eyes. I still could not quite believe her.

But that night I trembled with fear. It was around ten o' clock at night. When I heard a loud knock on the door, Amma panicked. She was just about to go to sleep.

"Open the door."

The words were washed out and slurred.

Startled, she froze.

"If you do not open the door, we will kick it in."

The banging on the door grew louder.

I thought it would break at any moment.

Amma went into the kitchen, got a cleaver knife and came to whoever might have opened the door.

The three men looked civilized. They were wearing trousers and shirts. The stocky, pot-bellied, balding man in the group had wobbly legs. The other two had also been drinking but had not lost their minds.

" Oh, did you want to sleep in peace and close the door after swindling our money? "

The fermented smell of alcohol emanated from the bald man's mouth and filled the room. As he tried to step into the house with his wobbly feet, Amma called out.

" Venu sir, take him away. If I owe you anything, I will repay it. If you come with these antics......."

Amma raised the cleaver in her hand to startle them.

He was slightly shaken, but it was no longer the smell of alcohol that came out of his mouth, but disgusting, foul words.

One of them tried to move him, but he tried to shake it off like an untamed bull. He continued his torrent of invectives.

"Oh, the queen is trying to scare me with a knife... Me of all people!"

He swayed and propped himself against the wall with one hand. I guess that's when he saw me, standing scared in a corner.

" Oh, the mother and daughter both deceived us and puffed up. "Amma lost her temper. As she tried to close the door, he pushed it open violently. With cleaver in hand and screaming, Amma jumped in.

"Get out of here. I am telling you to leave."

Her tone stunned him. She roared and stood there like rage incarnate. Our neighbours opened their doors to peep, but no one came to help us.

They slowly retreated as the melee continued. But the bald man continued to rain obscenities.

" We will never let you, mother and daughter, live in peace. We will never spare you. "

A shiver ran through my body. I wanted to run away, to escape it all, but the darkness outside frightened me. For the first time in my life, I was afraid of the dark. Frightened, I leaned against the wall.

The more fears sprouted in my mind, the less I could sleep. I tossed and turned in my bed. Whenever I tried to close my eyes tightly, I saw some kind of figures dancing in front of my eyes and I got scared. They might pounce on me with their tongues sticking out. When I opened my eyes, all I saw were lumps of darkness.

I had no idea what was going on around me.

Not knowing what to do, I spent the night.

Around eight o' clock I got up from my bed. I freshened up and as I walked into the hallway,

I saw a man with my mother. A short, bearded man. Both were deep in conversation. I turned around and went back to my room.

" Oh, Mole ... (dear child...) " I heard Amma call and turned to look at her.

" Come, sit here," she invited me politely.

I went over and sat on the chair opposite her. The long-bearded man smiled at me.

I feigned a smile. Amma introduced him to me.

" This is Shamsukkakka. His house is nearby. Owns a few shops in Bombay."

I sat there, uninterested.

" I told you yesterday that I did not want to involve you in my problems. Ikka (*Muslim elderly man*) told me that he will arrange a part-time job for you. Anyway, we have to leave here."

I lifted my gaze and looked into her eyes. Is she seeing things from my point of view? Does she care about my problems now? Or is this just her playing games?

My gaze revealed everything: panic, curiosity, fear.

She spoke as if her life had reached a point of no return. The thought of me being captivated by her problems worried her. The man Amma introduced as Ikka sat silently. It was as if Amma was speaking for him.

"For now, go to Bombay and take up work there. Later we will decide what to do."

Amma has already decided everything. She decides my life. She plans for my life, like an architect who can change his plan whenever he pleases.

The words of denial, like 'I do not want to go anywhere' stuck in my throat and never came out. Instead, I remembered the darkness that had frightened me last night. The figures with tongues sticking out, ready to devour me, lit up and flashed in my thoughts.

Away. Away somewhere.

A wind blew outside. The cold breeze that brushed through the rusty window grill of the train kissed my ear. Travelling with a man older than my father was unfamiliar, but it did not trigger any fear in me.

He was a man of few words. He was somewhat hesitant in his manner. At least that was the impression I got. I wanted to ask him what he did for a living and what kind of job he would get me in Bombay. But he didn't give me the leeway to ask these questions. Most of the time he stayed in the upper berth of the compartment. He got up on time to buy me something to eat. He enquired about my needs and bought it.

As the hours passed, the train covered long distances. New scenes. Unknown sky and unknown earth. Different life. In some places there were orphans, much like the streets of Calcutta. That hurt me. For a moment I thought of Thambikuttan. Poor boy! He's growing up ignorant of all this. In a way, his childhood is also wilting under the weight of the pain of being an orphan.

Sometimes the train went very fast, whistling, and at other times it was slow and groaning. The rhythm and speed of the train resembled human life. How long does the train take to reach its destination? How many hurdles does a human being have to overcome before he reaches his end?

My eyes followed him from the moment we boarded the train. He's the one who knows the destination of my journey. He's the one who should offer me shelter.

The train stopped in the big city of Bombay at midday, when the sun was burning mercilessly. The passengers were in a hurry to get off. He took the bag under the seat and asked me to get off.

From the female voice echoing through the public address system across the platform and the chunks of words on the display boards, I gathered that the station I was getting off at was called Victoria Terminus.

People were swarming everywhere. They moved busy and frantic. Every face showed a different emotion. Some, like me, confused at seeing the big city. Some were laughing or thinking. Some faces were somber and frozen in sadness.

I felt ashamed, thinking how small the world was that I had seen until then. How many people come to this city every day? They come from many different places. Each one of them could have a different story!

As I stood there with confused eyes, he tapped me on the shoulder to make me follow him. Not wanting to get lost in the melee, I tried to keep up with him.

For almost thirty minutes we went by taxi and he took me to a flat.

It was an old flat with narrow corridors. Only dim light. I felt crushed, as if I were crammed into a small room. A woman of almost fifty opened the door as Ikka knocked twice.

She was fair and plump. Her lips were red from lipstick. On both arms she wore red and green glass bangles. They tingled with the movement of her hands.

With a smile that showed her tobacco-coloured teeth, she invited us in.

"*Aavo beta. aavo.* Come in, my son. Come in."

Though I didn't know Hindi well, I doubted it because I knew the meaning of simple words like *beta* or *beti*. Doesn't *beta* mean son? Who had she called? Shouldn't she have called *beti* when it came to me?

While my mind was wandering, Ikka spoke to her in Hindi. Though I didn't understand much, I heard him address her as *deedi*.

" *Daro math, ye apki ghar jaise…....*
Don't be afraid, treat this house like yours..."

She said, taking my bag and placing it in the room.
My doubts disappeared when she called me *beti*.

" Let's stay here tonight. You must be tired from the journey. Freshen up and change your clothes." He said it with authority.

There was a visible change in the words and behaviour of Ikka who had been silent during the journey.

The lady led me to a room. She also showed me the toilet next to it. There she put my bag on a stool. As I stood there frightened, she came to me, held me by the shoulder and repeated her earlier words.

" *Daro math beti* …..... You don't need to be scared, daughter."

As she came closer to me, her plump bosom brushed my face. I turned my head away. From my shoulder, her fingers slid down my back, over my curves. Reluctantly, I slapped her hand away and backed away a little. Although she was a little annoyed, she smiled without hiding it.

" *Thu achee hum. Bahut khoobsurat lagti hum* …you're good. You look very beautiful."

With a sly, lascivious smile, she walked out of the room.

Her voluptuous body swayed to the rhythm of her feet. I locked the room as the ringing of her bangles died away.

Where am I?

I let my gaze wander around the room.

Sarees of various shades. *Dupattas, salwars* and *khameez* sets. In this room there were the dresses that girls wear. Also, a large dressing mirror. In front of it were powders, combs and other cosmetics.

Are all these hers? Did she have any daughters? What is her relationship with Ikka?

A parade of questions went on in my mind. I don't understand anything.

It's all jumbled up in my head. Seeds of fear began to sprout in my heart.

How could I begin this journey by trusting a stranger? What purpose did he find for me? I couldn't get out of the room, though I took a bath and changed. I thought these four walls would protect me. As I was tired from the journey, I lay down on the cot for some time. I think I slept for a while. I came to again when I heard a knock at the door.

"*Beti, darvasaa kholo* ... Daughter, open the door."It was the woman's voice. Her bangle began to jingle as she knocked on the door.

I felt that it would be of no use if I refused to open the door.

Although the fan was revving up, I continued to sweat.

I looked around the room. Is there any way to save myself? I was afraid even of my own shadow. When the knocking became loud enough to force the door open, I froze.

"Uma, open the door."

Still panicking, I removed the latch.

He pushed the door open and pushed his way into the room. As I stepped behind the door, he clutched my arms fiercely.

"What kind of nonsense are you doing? Is this how you behave in a house? Why are you being so disobedient?"

In his anger, his muscular hands pushed my arm down and it hurt. Again, I tried in vain to shake off his arm. He held my hand even tighter.

The woman standing outside came in and tried to placate him.

"*Are... beta..chod do... Ye chota ladki hena? Samachne ka time de do.*

Oh, my son... Let her... Isn't she a little girl? Give her time to understand." She came and took his hand from me. I lost control. The anger I was holding in my chest erupted.

"I don't want to stay here. You told me you'd get me a job. Please take me there. Or tell me where it's. I'll go there myself." He raised his right hand and wanted to slap me.

If the woman hadn't intervened, his hand would have fallen on me.

He hurled obscene words at me, his fiery eyes blazing with rage.

"You bitch, I brought you here for a job. Here, she'll tell you what your job is."

I was angry and sad and burst into tears.

While I was crying, I shouted,

"Let me go. Or I'll make a fuss here."

I grabbed my bag and tried to run out of the room. He tugged me by the arm and pushed me into the room. I fell and crashed face down. He yelled at me, unable to contain his anger.

"I've not paid your mother a rupee less than twenty thousand. How can I let you go without making it good?"

He broke off his words halfway and made a lewd sign.

I was stunned. Had this woman, my mother, sold me for a mere twenty thousand rupees? A kind of numbness spread from my head to my toes, like an electric shock. Had she tricked me by pretending to be guilty and remorseful?

Many questions and answers buzzed through my mind.

My heart was screaming. What will I do next? I continued to scream and cry. In the middle of it, the two of them were talking to each other. When he finally pushed her out and tried to lock the door, I gathered all my strength, pushed him away and ran out.

I ran and screamed at the top of my lungs. He chased me. I tried to enter the other flats, but none of the doors were open. While I was running, I knocked on several doors but none opened.

He muttered something and ran after me to catch up. I jumped down the stairs to save myself.

I had a strong feeling that I was on an adventurous tightrope walk between life and death. If I slowed down even for a second, he would catch up with me. That would mean my death. I ran with all my might through the dark corridor. I prayed fervently that a door would open for me. A prayer that did not work. As I ran from one block to the next, I saw two men going out and locking their doors.

I ran to them. I grabbed the hand of one of them and shouted for him to save me.

I gasped for breath. As my mouth had gone dry, I could say no more. I turned around and pointed my finger at them.

They froze in awe, not knowing what to do.

I looked behind me and pleaded with them with frightened eyes.

"He's going to hurt me. Save me."

Whether they understood me or not, they both stood paralysed.

I tried to speak to them in the Hindi and Tamil I knew.

" *Kaappathungo. Woh admi…….....* Save me. That, man..."

Before I could finish my words, the man caught up with me. He was a bit taken aback but changed his tactics.

" *Aavo beti, idhar nahee hai…….....*Come here, daughter. It is not here. "

As he walked towards me to grab me, I ducked behind them. Realizing that my fear and panic were increasing at the sight of him, one of them enquired about the details.

" *Ye kya he bhai… Ye ladki kai keliye ro rahaa hoon?*

Hey, what is this, brother? Why is this girl crying? "

He also replied something. I did not understand their conversation. I continued to shout loudly.

Hearing the noise, a man came out of the next flat and looked at me. As the crowd grew, Ikka came rushing over and pulled me by the arm. I shook him off.

"Save me. He is not with me. He offered me a job and brought me here. "

The man who came out of the flat last came up to me.

"Hey, Kuttee… (Kid)... What's the problem?" Hearing him speak Malayalam, I fell at his feet. As if finding a way to save myself, I opened up. Sobbing, I narrated all the events in one breath.

"Who are you? What do you want?"

He asked Ikka in a heavy voice. He ignored the question and tried to grab my arm again. The Malayali resisted. He seemed to have explained everything in Hindi to the other two. They too turned on Ikka.

Ikka was not ready to give up. They pushed and shoved each other. This led to a bigger squabble. As more people came, the situation got worse. I stood there, scared and shaking.

As he was beaten up more and more, Ikka shook himself off from them and ran away. Some chased him, beat him and kicked him again. Ashamed, I covered my face and cried.

"Now don't cry. Why did you come to a place like this with an unknown man?" Asked the Malayali who had saved me.

While suppressing my tears, I recounted what had happened. Before I could finish, I burst into tears again.

"Why are you crying now? Just think that you escaped only by luck." He placated me. He explained things to the others.

He left me in their company and went to call someone. The people who had gathered around me were sympathetic to my plight. I dared not look at anyone and sat there with downcast eyes.

He was from Thykkadu. His name was Gopi. Ten years ago, he left his home and came to Bombay. He took money from many people as an advance because a friend told him he would get them a visa for the Gulf countries. When the friend disappeared with the money, he had to flee.

When he came back after the phone call, he told me his story.

"This metropolis is like that. Thousands of people land here every day with great expectations. Some escape. Some fall into traps. Those who escape and those who are trapped will at least have another story to tell the world."

Although the heaviness that surrounded me did not leave me, his words were a relief. He handed me a bus ticket for the 9.30 pm bus to Thrissur and said,

"Third day, early in the morning you would reach Thrissur. I asked my brother Kumaran to come to the bus station.

He will be waiting for you there."

My face turned gloomy. I told him that I did not want to see that woman again.

"I will go to Sinthamanipudur."

"Once you reach Thrissur, you decide where to go. I would also feel relieved that I have kept you safe."

He offered me the ticket. Gratefully, I accepted it. I looked into his eyes with respect.

I wished I could tell him that he had given me my life back. But I held it all in a single glance.

"Do not remember what happened here."

With a smile he said.

That's right. I must believe that this phase of life did not happen at all. I must bury this in the inner chambers of my soul.

He asked the fellow passengers and the bus staff to take care of me as soon as he had said goodbye.

The bus left on time. In the glaring light of the sodium vapour lamps that turned the darkness into daylight, the hustle and bustle of the city of Bombay became very clear. The hum of the crowds. The hum of the vehicles.

I leaned back in my seat and closed my eyes. Restless thoughts condensed in my mind. I remembered Ikka and the other woman. Were they not the figures who came to devour me, with their tongues out?

SEVEN

Until a human being dissolves under six feet of earth, his life will go through several conflicts. Every human life ends up swimming in that murky ocean. When going through difficult situations, Thankamani's mother used to say that we have to bear them just because we are born in this world.

I too will bear them. But where will these difficult paths end?

Is there not an end to everything?

It was just morning. It was also very cold.

All the passengers had woken up before the bus reached the Thrissur bus station. In the midst of agonizing thoughts, I too had fallen asleep, but woke up quite early. As he said, Kumaran, Gopi's younger brother, was waiting for me. He was wearing a white dhoti and a checked shirt and looked very much like Gopi. Kumaran recognized me, perhaps because of Gopi's description.

"Aren't you Uma?"

As I looked around and got off the bus, he came up to me and asked.

I nodded yes. He introduced himself.

"I am Kumaran. Gopi is my elder brother."

I smiled as I understood him.

"Come, I will take you home."

Though I would have preferred to tell him that I did not want to go home, I obeyed him because I would have no answer if he had asked me where else to go.

Should I take a bus to Sinthamanipudur? That is the only way to escape. Or to Peace Home?

The Bishop told me that I can come back anytime... But,

A multitude of thoughts.

"Come, get in..."

As he told me, I got into the autorickshaw that was available. It drove off. No sooner had we covered a short distance than he slammed on the brakes and stopped.

The driver had halted when a van full of lambs going to the nearby slaughterhouse swerved right in front of him.

"Such a waste of time so early in the morning." he cursed under his breath.

My gaze shifted to the flock on the van. Their necks are gathered together and tied with a single rope. They are all standing head to head, rubbing shoulders. As if they were rubbing their cheeks together for comfort. Or are they exchanging their sorrows before the knife falls on them?

My mind raced as the autorickshaw approaches our house. How can I still face her after all this? Why should I have come to her after all I had been through?

The autorickshaw stopped in front of the house and I got out. He also got out with me.

I looked at him.

He understood what I meant, smiled and said,

"Call that woman. Let me see her."

As I stood there doubtfully, he whispered.

"*Ettan* (elder brother) told me everything. If there are such mothers in this world, I should not fail to see them. "

I knocked on the door.

There was no answer. Once again, I knocked.

I remembered that she had said she was moving away to ward off the people who had lent her money. As I stood there hesitating, he said to me,

"The house is locked. Shall we ask at the neighbour's house?"

I went to the house of Gracy Aunty. As soon as she found out that she had helped me to go to the Bishop's house, Amma quarrelled with Gracy Aunty. Since then, I could not bring myself to face her. Reluctantly, I arrived in front of her house.

"Oh, dear Uma."

With a broad smile, she invited me in. The same smile as before. Her demeanour told me that she was least upset about what had happened. I looked admiringly into her eyes. She inquired about my whereabouts.

"Come, what brings you here so early in the morning?"

"Is there no one here?" I looked towards the house and asked.

"Oh..., she is in the hospital. Yesterday morning she suddenly fell ill. Ramani, who works with her at the post office, told us."

I was lost in thought as I did not know what to do.

"Honey, come in."

"No, Aunty, let me go to the hospital and check."

I started walking from there. Kumaran was waiting for me outside. I told him the details.

In the same autorickshaw we went to the hospital. It was a new building constructed outside the city. Although it was still early in the morning, the grounds were swarming with people and vehicles.

We climbed out of the autorickshaw. It was not difficult to find the hospital. He was there with me. A dutiful younger brother was doing exactly what his elder brother had asked him to do.

Amma was admitted to the seventh room on the second floor. Since it was a new building, it was very clean. Both inside and outside. There was no pungent smell of medicines or other odours.

As we walked down the corridor, I saw a girl walking towards us with faltering steps, leaning on the shoulder of a middle-aged woman. Unable to bear the pain, she pressed her lips tightly together. This woman could be her mother. To relieve her, she stroked the girl on the back.

I imagined myself in her place. If I was in pain, whose shoulder would I lean on? Whose arms would caress me?

When we entered room number seven, she was lying on her side. A colourless liquid flowed into her vein through the tiny white tube from the dropper bottle hanging on the stand to the left of the bed.

What would her expression be when she saw me? Will it be surprise or anger? Or apprehension to learn how I had escaped? Whatever it was, I was eager to see it.

I moved in front of her like a victor. To show her that I had escaped, though she threw me at the feet of a bloodhound.

When she heard my footsteps, she turned her head and looked at me. She was stunned. Her eyes lit up.

"Uma, how did you get here?"

She did not finish her words and her voice broke. She tried to lean on her left elbow. She succeeded after some struggle. I stood still.

I was not sure what feelings were going on inside me.

She gave me a pitying look.

I was not sure whether to ignore it or get angry about it.

As she tried to sit up straight, she saw two eyes staring at her. Kumaran was watching her closely. She sat there with her eyes wide open, unable to recognise him. She was looking at both of us.

He certainly didn't want her to think too much as he introduced himself seriously.

" You wouldn't have recognized me. But I know you."

He paused and continued in a mocking tone.

"I do not know you fully. But I know that you are a strange mother. That is why I have come to see you."

She did not like his reproaching her.

"What do you mean? Who are you?"

She protested.

I was losing control. Until then I had been holding back, but then I blurted out as if I had got energy from somewhere.

"Whoever he is, who is this Ikka you sent me with? At what price did you sell me?"

"Are you my real mother? Can a mother sell her daughter?"

Though I was close to tears, I told her what I wanted to say.

I deliberately made sure my words sounded rude. Without understanding anything, she stared at me.

He too was watching her curiously. His voice rose when he saw that there was not even a trace of guilt on her face.

"You shouldn't have done so much cruelty to that girl. It is only her good fortune that she is back without any unfortunate incident."

He narrated whatever he had heard.

Her tired voice softened. Hurt, offended and dejected. Her voice was tired.

"I did not know anything. I sent her to him to get a job. I did not know he was such a scoundrel."

Her words were slightly shaky.

I looked at him.

An expression of annoyance and distaste remained on his face. She, unable to overcome the shock of our accusations, sat crouched in front of us like a puzzle.

EIGHT

It was night, but it was not dark around me.

But no light could tell me in which direction I should move to find a way out of my miserable life. My life resembled a ball of twine that became tighter and tighter the more I tried to untangle it. My life became a puzzle that became more and more complicated the more I tried to solve it. I felt suffocated, trapped in the shackles of adverse situations.

I was thrown into the drain of neglect and persecution.

Amma's stay in the hospital became a major turning point in my life's journey. The one who memorized *Bharathiyaar* poems and took an oath never to be a slave to a man, reciting lines aloud about women's freedom, had to lay down her body and soul before a man.

I trained my mind to be ready to return to Sinthamanipudur, or Bishop's house. It was unbearable for me to sit in the same room with her. I felt that the air in the room itself was polluted with lies. I do not know what effect my penetrating gaze had on her. But she wanted to say something. It was as if the stream of sound had dried up in her throat.

She sat up on her bed. There was a glass of water on the table beside her bed. As she drank the water, she gave me a pitying look.

Her look was interrupted when a nurse came in and pushed open the half-closed door.

After setting down her tablets and other medicines on the table, she handed me a bill and said in a serious tone.

"The doctor said it is possible to be discharged today. Pay the bill."

I stood there stunned for a moment.

The nurse was waiting impatiently to hand me the bill.

I looked at my mother doubtfully. There was an exasperated smile on her face.

The nurse's eyes moved from me to my mother and back again.

"Here, take it." Her tone became harder.

I regained my composure and took the bill.

She left the room muttering something unhappy.

I looked at the bill.

"*Mole...* (Dear child) ..." Amma's voice rolled over.

I lifted my face and looked at her.

My heart groaned with heaviness.

That she addressed me as '*Mole*' irritated me. I stared at the light beyond the room and stopped there.

"Uma, I do not have money to pay the bill. Let me give you a phone number. Someone will come with money. "

I looked at her as if I did not understand.

I was surprised that she could talk to me without guilt, even though she had caused me so much pain. I stood there not knowing what to do. I was in a daze.

I was careful not to give her any hint that I agreed with what she was saying.

"Two, sixty-seven, ninety-six."

She gave me the phone number.

I jotted it down in my memory.

Later these numbers became a part of my life.

"Call this number and say that you are calling on behalf of Thankamani. Premettan will take the call. "

I looked at her hesitantly as her words were full of confidence.

Though a question mark formed on my forehead, she said nothing more. Her words were full of confidence that he would lend a helping hand in any situation, no matter how difficult. I stared at her with mixed feelings of surprise, panic and contempt.

Who is he?

She smiled with a weak, fever-pale face.

A mysterious smile.

Or did it just seem that way?

The nurse, returning to fetch a tray she had left behind, inquired about the bill. I just looked at her innocently and said nothing.

Slightly annoyed, she walked out of the room.

"However vicious she may be, is she not the woman who gave birth to me? Let me do this to help her."

I said to myself.

"Does she deserve such kindness?"

Someone inside me wondered.

It was the first time I made a phone call. The cabin owner helped me dial the number. Though I said 'hello" in my panic, it still rang on the other end. In a shaky voice, I said "hello" again.

"Hello, who is it?"

The baritone voice on the other end of the phone made me even more nervous. I was at a loss for words. I remained silent for a moment.

"Hello, who is this?"

The voice on the other end became deeper and thicker. My ears were hurting. I struggled to recite what I had memorized.

"Is it not Premettan?"

"Yes, who is it?"

"I am calling on behalf of Thankamani, from Thahani Hospital. "

I finished in one breath. Were my words clear in my fright? Did he listen to what I said? But when I heard his reply, I realized that my doubts were unfounded.

"At the hospital? What happened? Who is this?"

Three questions at once.

I did not feel like talking any further. I have already said what I was confided in. I do not know how to explain further.

After a quarter of an hour he came. By then I had reached the room. Since he did not get any further details from me, he inquired about the room at the reception.

When he entered the room, he asked in an angry tone.

"Who made the call? Is that how you talk?"

I, who was sitting in the corner of the room with my head propped up on a table, raised my head and looked around.

A medium-sized, fair, bearded man. He was wearing a dhoti with coloured borders and a white shirt.

"Oh, has Premettan come?"

When Amma saw him, she looked excited and got up from the bed. He went to her and asked her the details of her ailment.

I was still standing there staring.

Somewhere I have seen this face before. Where did it come from?

My memories raced backwards.

Where did I see him?

My memories raced back to the last day of rehearsals for my mother's drama. Amma and I were both there, were not we? Were not there two eyes staring at me that day in the camp, in the dim light? The man blew out the smoke from the cigarette burning on his lips with a mocking smile.

Isn't this the same man?

To clarify my doubt, I observed him closely.

He hadn't combed his hair. His hair and beard had begun to grey slightly. Shining eyes.

He noticed that I was watching him. With his glowing eyes, he eyed me from head to toe.

"Wasn't it you who called?"

I didn't like the way he said 'you' in an authoritarian tone. I remained silent.

"Listen to me, Chechy."

He started talking to my mother.

"She hung up the phone without giving me any details.

The only thing she said was that she was calling on behalf of Thankamani........ and also, that she was calling from Thahani Hospital."

He turned to me and asked in a contemptuous tone.

"Do you want me to guess more details?

Is this the way you talk to others, Uma?"

I looked at him with great surprise when he called me by name. It was even more surprising that he called my mother 'Chechy'. Amma called him Premettan, and he called her Thankamani Chechy. It sounded strange.

"It's not wrong for you to say that her father spoiled her too much." When he said that, he stared at me and I couldn't stand it. I felt that I could no longer bear his stinging words and insults. As I was about to step out of the room, his baritone voice rose behind me again.

"Uma."

A shiver ran through my body.

There was a certain commanding power in that voice.

"You don't need to go anywhere now. I know what has to be done. Tomorrow I'll come. I need to talk to you."

I looked at him hesitantly. He repeated what he had said.

"Haven't you been listening to me? You wouldn't go anywhere. Neither to work nor to the bishop's house. Let's think about what to do."

I stood still. I didn't dare to resist his words. His voice was hoarse. His words were precise and measured.

They were strong enough to make me compliant.

He was almost my father's age and I had no idea what he had decided. It was he who paid the bill and took us to another house on rent.

As we drove past the bus station in his red Maruti car, my eyes fell on the roadside slaughterhouse. I averted my gaze when I saw the freshly cut head of a lamb dripping blood. The hanging pieces of meat also flashed before my eyes. As repulsive as it was, I looked again. I remembered the flock of lambs I had seen that morning. Which of them had been chosen to go under the knife? The lamb's head dripping with blood remained clearly in my mind.

Preman Thykkadu. That was the name by which he was known. A storyteller. He is also an aesthete by nature, devoted to culture and art. He owns a travel agency in Bombay. And rich.

I came to know these things through my mother's words. To impress me, she kept flattering him. I was not very interested. Besides, I did not want to talk to her. So, I did not seem to listen to her.

The next morning at six o'clock, his car came and stopped in front of our rented house, just as he had mentioned. The first thing I saw when I opened my eyes in the morning was his car.

"Girls should be obedient. I told you to get ready in the morning. "

As he got out of the car, my dishevelled look annoyed him.

With a serious look and firm steps, he came into the house and said,

"Get ready quickly. We have to go somewhere. I have something to tell you. "

I wanted to laugh. Without hiding it, I asked him.

"What do you want to talk about?" Even if there is something, let us sit here and talk."

Without letting the ridiculous smile disappear from my lips,

I said to myself.

"I am still not out of the trauma of being with a man like you."

I thought he had not heard. But his response was startling.

"I am not going to kill you or eat you."

After a moment of silence in which he stared at me, he continued.

"And no one will ever ask what your price is."

Questions surfaced in front of me again. How did he know what had happened? Or did it all happen with his knowledge?

What is he trying to say?

"Get ready. Let us go out and talk."

I stood there stunned as he continued to speak in his hoarse voice. I had no choice but to obey.

How many challenges have I overcome so far? Now I dare to tackle anything. The firm belief that I can overcome all adversities is now ingrained in me.

Within a few minutes I was ready and got into the car with him.

Daylight has just begun to spread. The area is just coming to its usual bustling life. I did not ask him where we were going or why we were going.

He drove the car at a moderate speed. If you look at the sides and sit in the back, the trees and the people move with the speed of dreams. I couldn't believe that it was my life without speed that moved faster than them.

The car that was driving with two silent beings stopped somewhere. I looked out the window to see where I was.

On all four sides the boundary walls were built high. We drove through the gate and went inside. Near the walls, there were bougainvillea plants whose flowers had fallen to the ground. From the first glance I knew it wasn't a house. He got out of the car and signalled me to come to him.

As I got out of the car, my eyes fell on the big red sign on the bright yellow tinted wall. I read it.

Victory Hotel, bar attached.

As I stood there reading, he walked in and sat down. I had to hurry to join him.

Without any fear, I sat down opposite him.

The staff at the bar knew him as a regular. So, they weren't surprised to see him so early in the morning. But they became curious about me. As their stares and low chatter increased, I felt harassed and asked him.

"What do you want to say? If you want me to talk to you here, it's not okay. "

He pretended not to hear me. I called the waiter and ordered his drink.

"If you need anything, please order."

I was annoyed at his words.

He stood at the bar early in the morning and asked me to order. The waiter stood there and smiled at me.

"I don't want anything."

I expressed my displeasure.

"An orange juice."

He brushed aside my objection and ordered.

There was silence for some time. We sat in silence, not looking at each other. The waiter brought the glass and the drink with ice cubes. When he had drunk half of the first peg, the orange juice was also brought. I glanced outside.

"Take the juice." He glared at me and said this very loudly. The waiters turned and looked at us when they heard it. He didn't care though. Who saw or who heard?

I swallowed the juice. I realized I was shuddering inside when he raised his voice. A strange fear came over me.

Maybe that's why I sit at the bar so early in the morning, unable to revolt.

He finished the first shot. As he poured the second, he smiled at me. It didn't suit him at all.

He threw two ice cubes into the glass with his fingers. They floated on top of the drink.

"Your mother might have told you about me, didn't she?" He asked in a calmer voice.

So, he knows how to talk like that too, I thought.

When I didn't respond to his question, his smile faded. His words became curt.

"Don't be silent, answer me."

As his voice grew louder, I nodded and said, "I know."

He continued with a low grunt.

"Your mother did the wrong thing. She shouldn't have trusted him and sent you alone with him to Bombay. "

The pauses between the sentences gave him a chance to gulp the liquor.

He tries to remind me of the things I try to forget. I would like to believe that such a day never happened in my life. Yet he said the same thing.

"Do not be afraid anymore. No one will come asking for you. No one will haggle over your price."

His words left me worried. But I dared not voice it. I sat idly by. He continued without looking me in the face.

"Do you know how much I paid for you? Fifty thousand rupees ... fifty thousand."

I sat there stunned. The glass of orange juice almost slipped out of my hand.

Unable to be convinced, I stared at him. Who had he paid fifty thousand to? Was she hawking me again? I wanted to scream. I felt I could not hold it in and would burst into tears. But I held on.

"Gopi, who saved you, contacted me first, from Bombay. He remembered me when he heard you were from Thrissur. That is how it happened. Shamsu, who brought you to Bombay, agreed to deliver you to someone for twenty-five thousand rupees. I paid double that to settle it."

As he told this like a story, I hung my head in humiliation. I did not understand everything he said.

Was he settling his bill for rescuing me? Or was he saying that I would become his slave for saving me?

"The settlement was not only for you but also for your mother's debt. She will be harassed no more. "

In short, he is the new saviour of my family, that's what he meant. As I listened to him, I felt no respect or reverence for him. His boastful words were unbearable to me.

I thought it was useless to remain silent. It is better to speak frankly. First, I must find out if he has anything more to say. I turned the glass of orange juice in my hand, gathered my courage and asked him.

"Is that what you wanted to say?"

He looked me in the eye dismissively. That was strong enough to take away the courage I had gathered.

When the ice cube tray was empty, he called the waiter. He gave him a look and showed him the empty tray. Submissively, he brought new ice cubes within no time.

As he turned to leave, he looked at my juice glass. It was still three-quarters full.

He kept repeating what he said. I was losing patience as

I sat there. Gradually the crowd at the bar grew. Not many could see us as we were sitting in a booth. Although he was emptying more and more drinks, it did not seem to intoxicate him. His words were still crisp and clear.

"So far I have spoken about you. About your safety. "When I looked at him listlessly, he continued seriously.

"Let me tell you something about me. I am married. I have a five-year-old daughter. My wife has cancer. I am looking for someone to take care of my daughter."

He talked quite openly and without reservation what he thought. I wanted to ask him why he did not get a nanny for his child. He continued as if my questions did not matter.

"There is a big age difference between us. But that does not matter. Just think of the security in your life now."

"That is ..."

Though I understood what he meant, I looked at him as if I did not know. When he understood the scorn in my voice, he became angry.

"It simply means that I want things to go my way."

With these words he emptied the rest of his glass.

I sat looking at him stoically. I am just old enough to be his daughter. And he is compelling me to live obeying what he says. But nowhere in the conversations did he say whether I should get married to him or live with him. So, what should I obey?

By the time we came out of the bar at noon, he was drunk.

But his words or deeds didn't betray the same. I thought the liquor did not affect his body at all.

When he dropped me off at home, he mentioned it again.

"Tomorrow morning, I will come. Be ready. "

Is it my duty to give him an audience for his drinking binge? Was he planning my secure life that way?

I spent that night thereafter making the strong decision that night that I did not need such protection.

The next day, without telling anyone, I took the bus to Sinthamanipudur. I must talk this out with my father and convince him. I must get a job somewhere. Or I must study further. A sense of insecurity forbade me. I wished I could sleep peacefully.

But destiny was not kind to me. Before I reached Sinthamanipudur, he had reached there by car, along with my mother. They'd have guessed that I wouldn't go anywhere else. He openly expressed his wrath toward me.

Since Achen had gone to Coimbatore for some work at the mill, I couldn't meet him. Left without a choice, I had to yield to their threat. I will spend the rest of my life under the horizon of security that he has offered me. Or, end my life believing that I was destined to live only until now.

I didn't have the courage for the latter. I must live and face my challenges until my last breath. I shouldn't lose my strength in challenging situations.

Somewhere, there is a written destiny.

There is no use living indifferent enough to sacrifice oneself.

That strong conviction made me myself.

NINE

Someone unknown to me wrote everything into my destiny. I was forced to live by it.

Unofficially, I had become Preman's wife. He always took me to the bar and into his art and social circles. Although he often said harsh words, there were no unacceptable obscene words or actions from him. Slowly I overcame the initial discomfort. I began to get used to it. Every day he would take me either to the bar or to his office in Thrissur. He started entrusting me with some simple accounts of his office in Bombay to manage. The impression was that he was taking me along as his secretary.

His friends included many prominent personalities in the field of arts and culture, including film director Pavithran and writer Chintha Ravi. By then, I was already known as Preman's wife in the eyes of his friends and the locals. I did not try to correct them. In a way, I too began to feel secure in the horizon he had created for me, as he once said. The making of a documentary film paved the way for me to move from secretary to his wife.

Preman produced the documentary titled "*Kallinte Kadha* (The Story of Toddy)", which Pavithran directed.

It was a film to show the history and greatness of Toddy, the alcoholic drink made from palm trees.

Preman, who always created 'suspense' in life, suddenly told me about it.

That evening he dropped me at home.

"Kuttee... (Child)"

Sometimes he called me that. Very rarely... It was gentle... That day too, when I heard that honey-coated name,

I turned around.

" Tomorrow we are going away... We will not be back for a week. Take clothes for a week. "

It tickled my tongue to ask him where.

It was a question that sprang from my restlessness. But the expression on his face kept me silent. He must also feel that it is important for me to know where I am going or why I am going.

One who is destined to obey

One who is destined to obey his orders

Slave

Whatever words you use

I made another synonym

The next day, as he had decided, I packed for a week and went with him.

It was not a long journey. We went to Hotel Elite in Thrissur, which was only a few kilometres from home.

I was not surprised because hotels and bars were nothing new to me. But I wondered why it was necessary to stay in a hotel in Thrissur itself.

Although he could see my doubts clouding my eyes, he said nothing.

The gravity of the situation became clear when I saw Pavithran, Chintha Ravi and a few others at the reception.

They were about to start shooting for the documentary.

The stay at the hotel was for preparations.

After greeting each other at the reception and collecting the keys, they went to their rooms.

Preman, who took me to Room No. 203, was excited as I looked at him in confusion. He brought in our bags, put them in a corner and came towards me. He looked at me mockingly.

"This room is for you. I will go to the others, somewhere there."

Unknowingly, a sigh escaped me. He became angry when he noticed it.

" Are you afraid to share the bed with me? To the others you are now the wife of Preman, remember that. "

When he looked me in the eye and said that, I hung my head.

'Wife' - hearing that word scared me.

I had the urge to tell him that I did not harbour that desire. And that the others should keep their ideas to themselves.

But,

Fear... I did not dare contradict him. The fire in me had burnt out. I got used to living in the safety net he created for me.

But things turned out differently than he had told me.

In the room set up for me, their discussion on the 'Story of Toddy' took place.

In the evening, all his friends came to the room. They started the discussion. They also made the shooting location plan and schedule. I stood there listening to conversations I could never understand. The liquor was flowing while they discussed toddy's story. I was the only woman there. But those who were drinking did not think about the fact that I was also in the room. They celebrated the discussion with roast buffalo and chicken. As it went on, I wanted to run out of the room. Being used to only vegetarian food, the smell of meat, fermented drinks and cigarettes made me feel sick. They ignored my discomfort, ate and drank and made fun. I tried to control my churning stomach by shutting my mouth tightly, but lost control once. I ran to the toilet.

I closed the door and sat there for some time.

By now the alcohol had taken effect in them and the conversations digressed from toddy to many other topics. They also started describing women. I did not understand much of it.

When the din died down, I came out of the toilet. Some drunks had already started sleeping there. The cot was meant for two people, but four or five were sleeping on top of each other. I thought only the empty liquor bottles and I could stand up straight. I left the men to their fate and spread a bed sheet on the floor. In the corner of the room I slept, covered like a pile of clothes.

When I opened my eyes in the morning, there was no one in the room. The leftovers from the night, empty glasses and bottles and rubbish were scattered all over the room. A foul smell filled the room. I rinsed all the glasses. I put the empty bottles in a plastic bag and threw them in the rubbish bin. As I was cleaning the room, Preman came in.

" Aren't you done yet? It's time to start shooting."

I was stunned to see him talking seriously as if nothing had happened. Is this the same person who drank and partied till dawn?

Did he ever think that I, another human being, was in that room?

I have more questions to ask. But whom should I ask?

Or who should ask?

I felt strong contempt for myself as I felt myself losing my ability to react. I cleared all the leftover food and rubbish from the room and tidied up. After taking a bath, I got ready and went to the shooting hall. Everyone was very excited. It was as if they had nothing of the previous night's events in their minds. For them it could be routine. Since it is not routine for me, I find it unnatural. Even otherwise, I'm traveling weird paths of life now!

On the following days, the events of the first day of 'The Story of Toddy' repeated. 'The room set up for me' became their safe place. I and the four walls were silent witnesses to everything. The responsibility entrusted to me was to keep a record of the shooting expenses.

I did it very well.

We stayed at Elite Hotel and shooting the movie for almost six more days. The next day we were to move to Padiyoor near Irinjalakkuda. Around noon, the troupe left Elite Hotel and went to Padiyoor. We stayed at the hotel with Pavithran, two of his assistants and two others. In the afternoon, they started drinking. That day they were all together in Pavithran's room drinking. I locked my room and lay down to sleep. When I woke up, I heard Pavithran's assistant calling for me.

" They told me to ask you to come quickly to their room.

"He finished the sentence and hurried away. Without

having a clue, I followed him.

I was shocked to see Preman in the room covered in blood. A fly was resting on his beard, soaked with blood. I shooed it away. I wiped his face with a towel.

By this time a taxi had been ordered to take him to the hospital. As they helped him into the car, Pavithran said, to no one in particular,

" It's nothing serious, maybe it's due to lack of sleep."

I don't know if he said this to reassure himself or someone else. I didn't pretend to hear it. Many times, I had noticed his unusual coughing during conversations. I saw him stroke his chest with the palm of his right hand as if he was afraid his chest would burst. Then his face contorted as if he was struggling to swallow saliva even.

The pain or discomfort he felt in such situations never worried me.

I felt no pity for him. But now...

The car sped to the hospital.

He sat upright with two tablets and an injection. The doctor made a note of some urgent tests and said,"Have him admitted for two days. We'll discharge him when we've seen the test results. "

Preman and Pavithran looked at each other. Though Pavithran agreed, Preman protested to the doctor in his exhausted voice.

" That isn't possible, doctor. We're busy with some urgent matters. I've to be discharged today."

The doctor pretended to smile at him. Pavithran looked at me as if he wanted my opinion. I kept my face down as I had no opinion or position on the matter.

As no one agreed with what the doctor said, he continued seriously.

" There are signs of TB. The two tests are to confirm that. If you want, you can go. But if you're careful now, problems can be avoided. "

The doctor looked at me as if he were talking to me.

"Don't drink any more alcohol. It's of utmost

importance that those who live with the patient must be careful. Since germs are spread through the air, one shouldn't have close contact with the patient. Eating from a plate that the sick person has used should also be avoided."

When Preman heard the doctor's words, a smile appeared on his face. A crooked smile.

It was pointed towards me.

I stood leaning against the wall, like a statue. Ignoring the doctor's words, we immediately returned to the hotel. During the journey, Preman opened his mouth only to taunt the doctor.

As soon as we reached the room, they gathered again to drink. Although the doctor had advised against drinking, Preman joined them. Those who drank with him didn't advise him against it, but said words of encouragement.

One said,

" Doctors tell us many stupid things. There are so many cases where medical science has failed. We'll defeat them in Preman's case too. "

Excited by his words and his overflowing love for a friend, others embraced him. One man kissed him. Pavithran's assistant was more self-sacrificing.

" Today I'll eat only from Premettan's plate. "

He put his hand on the plate Preman was using. I wanted to laugh out loud. How mad a man can be when intoxicated! I was a silent witness to all this.

I thought his friends were ready to die for him. Is this real love? Is it?

The effect of the stimulating chemicals flowing in their veins?

Though the friends were ready to give their hearts for him, he came to me indifferently.

The wild look in his eyes frightened me.

With his arm sliding through my shoulder, he pulled me close.

His beard scratched my cheek. Disgusted, I turned my face away. It displeased him.

Like a little kitten scruffed by a mother cat, he pulled me towards him.

His friends laughed at the sight.

When a cat tries to catch a mouse, it is a pleasure for it to see the mouse trying to escape. But for the mouse it is a great agony.

I writhed in the same pain.

Preman enjoyed the sight and called out to his friends.

" She is my *Thanka kutti* (golden girl). "

He winked and stopped halfway.

With a hearty laugh, an assistant filled him in.

" That meant, the child of our Thankamani. "

The audience laughed uproariously.

I tried to tear myself away from his hands.

But my body slackened in its strength.

He heaved himself forward with me, took the plate he was eating from and continued.

" Today we will both eat from the same plate. That is, she will eat from the plate I ate from. "

Intoxicated as he was, he took a cube of meat from the plate and brought it to my mouth. I closed my eyes tightly as his fingers dipped into the pickle and the meat curry came close to my mouth. I clenched my teeth tightly to keep my mouth from opening. Forcefully, he tried to push the meat into my mouth. I was on the verge of vomiting. I cried out loudly, "I am not eating this... I do not want to... "

No one heard me cry. There was loud laughter around me. Someone was mocking me.

" Oh, she is from the royal family... She is not allowed to eat meat! "

They roared with laughter.

Once again, I tried to protest.

That failed too. With force, he shoved a piece of meat into my mouth. Disgusted, I tried to spit it out, but he covered my mouth with his hand. As I gagged, my eyes bugged out. Someone, sensing trouble, intervened.

" Leave her, Preman. She is not mature... That's the reason. "

Though he stopped in the middle,
he added a veiled statement and finished.

" You would have to teach her everything,
chinna ponne..(you little girl). "

The others continued to howl.

I freed myself from Preman's arms. To spit out the meat,
I ran into the washroom.

I spat it out.

The smell of the spices remained in my mouth despite washing several times.

I looked at my face in the mirror in the washroom.

I felt that my reflection was mocking me.

I was angry.

The anger rose like an ocean.

I took a sip of water and spat at my reflection.

Not just once...

Many times,

Until my anger dissipated.

The next morning, when we left the hotel and moved to Padiyoor, Preman made a long face.

The others seemed unmoved. I had the feeling that these people never want a stain of their past to stick to their chest of memories.

The attitude of repressing yesterday's events was then itself.

What should I do to forget everything?

We reached Padiyoor to take up '*Kanalattam*' and were accommodated in a rented house there.

He did not speak to me either during the journey or after we reached Padiyoor. I saw him looking at me with sympathy, at times.

Perhaps he also felt guilty.

What is the use of apologizing to people who would stop at nothing under the influence of alcohol?

In the evening, they started preparing for *Kanalattam* (a devotee dancing on live coals) in the courtyard. Preman and his friends began their 'programme" as if they had decided not to record *'The Story of Toddy'* without alcohol.

Unlike in the hotel room, they were not very strident.

I thought it was wrong to say that alcohol erases ideas of situation, background or personal qualities.

I do not know how long I sat in that room.

When I saw the light of the smouldering coals in the fireplace, I held on to the window bars and watched the preparations outside.

When I heard someone close the door, I turned around.

It was Preman. With him came the unpleasant smell of alcohol.

He came close to me.

Although he was heavily drunk, his gait was steady.

His eyes were red.

No one would dare if he harmed me.

I do not have the strength to resist him. So, he can do anything.

I am ready.

I stood there without any panic.

" Kuttee (child)…"

He called me softly.

I lifted my face and looked at him.

From the pocket of his kurta he took out a gold chain and handed it to me.

Hanging from it was an *Alilatthali* (ficus - leaf shaped pendant that married woman wear).

"Wear it around your neck. You can proudly tell others

that you are my wife. "

These words were full of arrogance.

I can proudly say that I am Preman's wife, it seems.

I wanted to laugh. Do I have to wear the *thali* necklace he brought myself to confirm my right?

The people around me, the relatives and his friends, believe that I am Preman's wife.

Who else would know?

With whom should I confirm my rights?

My tongue knew only too well that I had no right to ask questions. Instead of these questions, I said something else.

" I have no need of it.

I do not wear jewellery."

My defiant voice annoyed him.

His composure suddenly faded. He gritted his teeth and flew into a rage.

" Take this. If you are Preman's wife, live by his status, this is not your *Pandi* (Tamilian) colony."

How despicable he made the word '*Pandi* colony' sound.

This was my heaven.

I lived there as myself. Only there.

I had dignity, self-esteem and courage...

And now...

" Take this." offering me a necklace, he said rudely to me.

He was very careful not to let the shouting outside be heard.

I looked again at the golden chain and the *Alilatthali*.

I sensed that the *Alilatthali* was in the shape of a woman.

A yellow rope attached to her neck...

A woman's body hanging on a rope...

I took the chain from him.

When he faced me, he was the conqueror. Whenever I gave in, he was satisfied.

The behavioral disorder of deriving happiness from cruelty!

Outside, they started *Kanalaattam*. The beat of the drums became faster.

Along with it, the jingling of anklets. With a yell, a figure ran into the fire pit. The roar and the rhythm echoed in my ear.

I looked up into his face. His eyes were as red as the embers outside.

He stood there, more fearsome than the figure executing *Kanalaattam*.

I adorned myself with the *thali* and watched the fire burning outside the window at man height. Outside, the screams and thuds reached their climax.

While I wore the chain, he left the room like a man enjoying a wild sport.

As he walked out like a champion, he turned and looked at me.

I saw an enigmatic smile in his eyes. I felt nothing more than the added weight of the thali chain to make people believe that Uma Devi was Preman Thykkad's wife.

I watched the scenes outside.

The man playing *Kanalaattam* ran back into the fire pit.

For a moment he disappeared into the pile of glowing embers.

The fire blazed at the height of a man. It wavered like my mind.

    ....

That night we finished shooting *Kanalaattam* and went to the Parassinikkadavu Muthappan temple.

The shooting continued there for almost a week.

The editing took place at Chithranjali Studio in Thiruvananthapuram.

When he left the rest of the work to Pavithran, he asked me to prepare for another trip. This trip was to Bombay.

I followed him like an obedient sheep.

We reached Bombay at dusk.

The city of Bombay...

The place that gifted me with experiences I never want to recount.

I never thought I would ever set foot in the same city from which I had escaped with someone's help.

Fate brought me back there.

We came to the two-room flat in the CGS quarters of Koliwada.

It belonged to him. Another stifling flat with dark corridors surfaced in my memory.

No.

It was not the same...

It was tidy. Full of light... And big.

I liked the flat with all its amenities.

I opened the window in the hallway and went out onto the balcony.

On the other side, another building was under construction. Two bright eyes watched me from this area filled with bricks,

granite blocks and cement dust.

They were the eyes of a kitten curled up on the edge of a wooden ladder.

I too stared back.

Poor thing. It closed its eyes.

I stood there and watched it.

I felt it was gripped tightly by fear.

At a soft sound it jumped up and prepared to flee. Something is scary there, I guessed.

What could it be?

In Bombay, Preman behaved differently.

No trace of the seriousness.

Calm demeanour. Mild conversation.

His clothes were different too. He, who always wore dhoti and kurta in Kerala, switched to jeans and shirt. His drinking habits did not change. Since I was not allowed to, I did not comment on such things.

His coughing fits were getting worse, indicating that his health was deteriorating day by day.

Although the doctor had warned against close contact with others, to challenge medical science or not, I am not sure, we slept in the same room. For the first two or three days he tried to forcefully satisfy his lustful desires on me, but his physical condition did not allow it.

I let it all wash over me and thought that my life, both my body and my mind, were enslaved by him.

Still, I had some hope that my dark journey would end. I dreamt of a light shining brightly somewhere. I was condemned to a kind of solitary confinement in the Bombay flat. Early in the morning Preman went to his office and returned late at night. There was no one I could talk to.

There were strict instructions that I was not to befriend anyone. Nevertheless, from the balcony I looked hopefully at the next one. That maybe I would see another woman... to smile, to get acquainted with her.

I never saw anyone outside.

There was a greengrocer's shop just below the flat. There were other shops nearby where you could buy all the essential groceries. He bought them.

I was rarely allowed to do that. Then language became a barrier.

Whenever I got the rare opportunities to speak, I tried my best to speak.

Otherwise I might even lose my ability to speak, I thought.

Sometimes I also talked to the walls.

Even though they did not respond, they heard my story.

One day, when I was alone talking to the walls, this Preman came in.

No sooner was he in than he searched the room. He suspected I was hiding someone. Not only that day, but also on the following days, his paranoid suspicions grew. He did not let me go to the balcony and did not buy vegetables. One day I saw him searching for my lover in the house and when he came back from the office, I lost my temper and exploded.

" Who are you looking for? This has been going on for so many days now. Didn't you catch him? "

He could not bear the despair and contempt in words. In a fit of rage, he moved closer to me and raised his arm to slap me.

I stood like a rock without hesitation.

" Yes, I am looking for 'the other'. I do not trust you. You are that woman's daughter. "

I felt numb from the toe up.

" *Endee Uma. Avan sonnathu ennaannu puriyaathaaa.unka* Amma *palalisaamy koode odippoya maathiri neeyum yaarkoodeyaavathu odippoyiduviyaa* ......

Uma, did you not understand what he said? Just as your mother eloped with Palaniswamy, you too will elope with someone, it seems..."

I felt Thankamani step in front of me and tell me that.

The narrow path of Sinthamanipudur appeared before me.

I remembered what Mani from Palakkad had said,

"*Amma ettadi paanjaa makaa pathinaaradi paayum* ... Like a daughter, like a mother."

He said something with the same meaning. You are the daughter of the same mother, are you not?

I did not understand it then.

Now I understand it, but I cannot respond to it.

" I am sure that you have never lived with anyone.

To confirm it, I took the virginity test... "

I felt like the world was spinning around me.

As if my legs had become weak. I wished the earth would give way... and I could disappear.

When we returned from Parassinikkadavu after shooting the documentary, he went with me to a hospital in Calicut. He told me that he wanted to meet a doctor friend of his. On the way back, although it was late, I could not remember anything. Now I realized that they had done a virginity test while I was unconscious.

Humiliation, anger and indignation ... rose up inside me.

I wanted to punish myself by jumping off the building.

Or, Should I strangle his neck...

The flames of anger spread from my eyes to his and he lost his temper and became furious.

He pointed his fingers at my face.

" I will scratch out your eyes, you... How she stares!"

As he said this, his saliva splashed from his mouth into my face. Annoyed, I wiped it away with my palm. Seeing this, he became even more piqued, coughed up more phlegm and spat in my face.

" Wipe it away. I am terminally ill. Wipe it off. "

It was obvious that he was tormented by feelings of inferiority. His physical illnesses and sexual dissatisfaction were behind his words and actions.

He muttered something and left the room.

I looked at myself in the mirror.

His spit dripped from my right cheek. His mucus stuck to many places on my face.

I felt disgusted with myself.

But I did not cry.

I am his slave.

The owner can do anything to a slave.

Spit on, beat or even kill.

Who says slavery is over?

In many places, people make slaves out of people.

Is that not so?

Similarly, I am also a slave.

I am obliged to listen to and obey my owner who protects me.

That night he had drunk too much. The guilt had begun to sting him. It is foolish to think that Preman Thykkadu would admit his wrongdoing or apologize.

Late that night he came to my bedside and put his hands around me. Although I felt like I was suffocating, I gave in to him. When he brought his mouth, with which he had spat at me earlier, close to my face, I felt gagged.

His strength wore me down. He completely subdued me.

The next day, when I got up, my body ached in many places. When I got up, he was ready to travel and was wearing a dhoti and a kurta. He had also packed four or five pairs of clothes in his briefcase.

He had the look of a warrior who has won a battle. With a slight smile, he said,

"I will not be here for a week. I have bought the necessities for a week.

If you need anything else, you can call Kareem."

Kareem was his business partner in Bombay.

He locked the door from the outside and left.

I was allowed to enter the balcony, which was only half a metre wide, to enjoy the air and light from outside.

I went out onto the balcony.

On the opposite side, the construction of the building was going on rapidly.

My gaze grazed the wooden ladder.

No. It was not there.

I looked for it everywhere.

Where had the grey cat with the bright eyes gone?

TEN

In this world there are only two kinds of people - those who have money and those who have none.

All other divisions are based on this money. Looking at Preman's life, I think those who have money value it only as paper. They do not mind throwing away the paper to possess or enjoy something they crave. They do it while those who do not have money understand the true value of money and join the race to earn it.

Preman had a lot of friends. Most of them were from the film or theatre world. He enjoyed spending his time with them. I remained a spectator at many of his liquor parties. But such events were rare in the Bombay flat.

But sometimes Preman would host visiting artistes from Kerala there. At such parties for his close friends, liquor was the main lure. It was at one of these parties that I heard his philosophy on money.

"Money can buy everything in this world."

"I have money. So, I will get what I want. "

I heard this story while shooting for the Malayalam film '*Indrajalam*'. I, who usually watched only Tamil films, did not know any Malayalam film stars. On that day, a few of these stars were in the flat. As the party continued with music, dancing and drinks, someone wished to go to the dance bar to watch cabaret. Preman Thykkad, wanting to fulfil his friend's wish, took them to one of the most opulent dance bars in Bombay. Unfortunately, one person in the group was wearing a dhoti, a kurta and slippers, and they were not allowed in.

A scuffle broke out in the dance bar because of this silly incident.

Preman Thykkad was not ready to take insults lying down. It is said that he paid the leading dancer of the bar ten thousand rupees, took her to Juhu Beach and made her dance in public. That was Preman Thykkad. Life held a great lesson for him, who blindly believed that there was nothing that money could not buy.

In the meantime, some other important events happened.

In January 1991, the shooting of the film *Bali* directed by Pavithran began. We came from Bombay to Thrissur for the shooting.

During the journey, I was constantly tired and felt dizzy. I thought it was because of the journey. I went to the nearby hospital with Preman as I was experiencing some unusual symptoms.

I sat there stunned and listened to what the doctor had said. My doubts were confirmed. But for any other woman, those words would have given life a deeper meaning.

"You are going to be a mother."

But were those words strong enough for me to make me happy? How could I, carrying the burden of loneliness, be a good mother? Should the child share the agony I go through?

Preman might have sensed my helplessness because he gave me a mocking smile.

The smile of a champion.

He used to take me to the filming locations. Sometimes I thought he wanted to show people that he had a youthful wife. But this time it turned against him.

On the set, Preman's real life exposed itself before my eyes. He betrayed me.

Everything he told me about his life was a lie. That he told me his wife had cancer and he had only one daughter was only a small part of the big lies he told me.

He had three wives.

Radha, Santha and Nirmala.

He divorced Radha a long time ago. Then he married Santha. She lived in his house in Guruvayoor.

The third, Nirmala, is in Bombay. I am his fourth wife.

I was disappointed that I kept being led by the nose.

First by my mother. Now by the man who offered me shelter.

I wept bitterly as I could not control my grief. I was ashamed of his life that was germinating inside me.

For a moment I considered killing this one-month-old life and running away from life itself.

But I could not retreat defeated. I cannot live sobbing and grieving. I am not ready to leave this world. When he realized that I had come to know everything for the first time, he asked me to forgive him.

"I could not tell you earlier. That was my mistake. I thought your mother had told you everything."

Without saying a word, I stood before him, impassive and

lost as I was.

They would not have kept quiet to hide things from me. His friends would have thought that Preman had sacrificially given me life.

Preman would have become an icon of kindness for giving life to an orphan girl.

When we returned to Bombay, I had made up my mind.

I would live with him, look after his office and take care of his medicines.

Beyond that,

I would never share a bed with him.

That was my firm decision.

I wanted him to think that I was punishing him in the least possible way.

My revenge for being betrayed.

It was my situation that made me live even in the exhausting desolation I was experiencing in my flat in Bombay. The building across the road was ready in almost ten months. I calculated that exactly.

That is the time when the sperm sown by Preman grows inside me.

During my pregnancy, I longed for someone to support me.

But there was no one.

Meanwhile, Amma was living in a rented house in Kechery. This house was also arranged by Preman.

In September, persuaded by Preman, she came to live in the Bombay flat. I think he sent for my mother because he saw my distress. But her presence annoyed me more.

Even as I writhed in pain and gritted my teeth, I endured. On 21 September, in the early hours of the morning, the contractions got worse and worse. I cried out in pain.

As if the baby was desperate to get out of the loneliness of my womb, it stuck the head out. I was admitted to the Seethalekshmy Maternity Nursing Home in Koliwada.

Motherhood increased my pride in my womanhood.

I became a mother.

A baby was born for me in my blood.

He will be everything for me.

I am no longer alone.

He is my everything-in-everything.

I am no longer alone.

From now on, my life belongs to Him.

Sharath, my beloved son.

In his playful laughter I searched for the essence of my life. Every moment I lived for him.

I was amazed at how Preman showered Sharath with love and care. How many faces can one person have? How can such a soft-hearted person behave so wildly towards me?

Three months later, Amma returned from Bombay.

Her presence did not reassure me in the least.

She pretended that Preman had persuaded her to come, but the truth was different.

But such thoughts did not affect me. My life was changing. I realized it was a change through motherhood. I was freed from my loneliness. In its exuberance, I tried to forget my past.

Though we first went to the house of Preman's ancestors, later we moved to the house in Guruvayoor, heartbroken by his sister's biting words.

She would have been upset when she saw the number of her brother's wives increasing. She made fun of us and even claimed that Preman was living with a mother as well as her daughter. This opinion could be based on the fact that she does not tolerate her brother's money being shared by many.

Whatever the reason for this emotional outburst, these filthy words seemed to engulf me. Even though I try to wash them off, the foul smell of those words does not seem to disappear.

We started living with Santhechy in Guruvayoor. She was the embodiment of peace, just like her name. She believed that a woman must be tolerant and forgiving of everything, and she spent her days without complaints or quarrels.

I was not like that.

I shrunk my relationship with Preman to that of a secretary, a housekeeper or a manager.

That was the inferno of revenge in me. I made sure it never burnt out.

But in return I had to endure his brutal torture.

ELEVEN

That day I noticed a change in Preman's behaviour since he had come from Bombay that afternoon. He was sitting in an armchair on the veranda, talking to no one and staring into the distance. I did not dare ask him anything.

For several months we had talked about nothing but accounts. I sat down on my bed, under the fan, with a half-read magazine. If I sat directly under the fan, the breeze would fall on me. I just wanted to get comfortable in the hot weather.

I was engrossed in my reading. After a while I heard the door close and I raised my head and looked around.

Preman was standing right in front of me, with a determined look. There was an unusual ferocity in his eyes. Although I was startled, I did not let it show. I stared at him gallantly.

The rest went quickly. From the clothes in the room, he took a churidar shawl and tied my hands to the posts of the cot. Though I tried to jump up, his manly arms overpowered me. I tried to call out loud for Santhechy. He stuffed a piece of cloth in my mouth. I was gagged. He behaved like a wild animal.

Have I lived with such a man for so many years? He tried to penetrate me with all his might.

I jerked in pain and tried to shake him off. He pressed into me and shouted.

" Didn't you want to test me, to take revenge on me? You, a woman, can never settle a score with a man."

That was his inhuman judgement on me for refusing to sleep with him. Later he mentioned it. It was Kareem Ikka who advised him to use force against me. But he was not in control of things.

He panicked when I was lying on the floor bleeding. He was stunned and did not know what to do. My eyes were half closed. He removed the cloth from my mouth, opened the door and went out. I was half unconscious and could feel the blood congealing on my body.

When I opened my eyes, I was in the hospital.

The doctor insisted on not treating me until a complaint was made to the police. She wanted to ensure that such atrocities were punished. My condition was pathetic. I had lost blood and fainted. I had severe pain all over my body. I went to the hospital where my wounds were stitched.

With an apology to the doctor that it was a slip by my husband, we were able to avoid police intervention. He too was of the opinion that it was a thoughtless and absurd behaviour.

When I opened my eyes, the first thing I saw was his face, tense and strained. There were dark circles around his eyes. Those eyes kept looking at me pleadingly, as if begging for forgiveness.

I tried to smile. That smile told him something.

Decide for yourself the penance to forgive your sin.

Realize the depth of the agony you perpetrated.

Unable to look at him any longer, I hid my face under the blanket.

TWELVE

Nothing is predetermined. When I opened the pages of my life story, it was all fate, unknown.

My family life lasted seven years. There were no common interests between us. A married life to stay away from each other. After that assault, his behaviour changed subtly. Was it guilt or remorse? I am not sure. He approached me in a gentle way.

I described myself as a secretary or manager, keeping a close watch on his accounts and giving him his medicines on time.

In the meantime, Amma had found a job abroad with Preman's help.

During this time, my father's passing away saddened me immensely.

It was a heart attack. I cried a lot and remembered him as a person who carried all his sorrow.

My father was very unhappy at the thought of my fate. He expressed it when we visited him once in Sinthamanipudur.

"Preman, how can you consider a girl of your daughter's age as your wife?"

He asked in his heavy heartbreak.

But Preman's reply was very rude. He became very angry. He used many foul words. He went out of the house swearing, taking me along. When I looked back, my father was still standing in the portico, his eyes moist.

My father's death left a big gap in my life. A man who lived like a whirlwind; my guru who taught me the first lessons of social service. His visits to the Gounders' homes and residential colonies remain in my memory.

They are all memories. In the meantime, Preman's illness worsened. His cough became violent.

He spat blood regularly. He did not stop drinking even as his pain worsened.

Under my duress, he consented to a more detailed examination. It was not the typical TB, but multi-drug resistant tuberculosis that had affected him. The treatment would have been better if we had known earlier. He took medication for TB for several years. In reality, he never tried to understand his real situation and scoffed at the fact that medical science can fail.

When the disease finally took over his body and mind, he was ready to do anything to save himself. He was treated at the Sree Chithra Medical Centre in Thiruvananthapuram. One of his lungs was surgically removed. He insisted that I should stay with him in the hospital. I did.

For ninety-six days he was on a ventilator. He had a pathological fear of death. He was prepared to spend all his money to keep himself alive. It was one of those moments when a person realizes how foolish it is to believe that money can buy everything. Diseases and medicines expose the frivolity of human life.

But he was able to delay his death with his money. He was on a ventilator for ninety-six days. This is what he insisted on. In his fear of death, he hinted at it.

At that time, the doctors said there was not much to hope for. The disease had progressed much.

"Uma, I have not given you a life to be happy about. I have done things that are not worth remembering. Leave me like this. I have earned enough money. Let me keep my breath while it lasts."

As he said this, taking a laboured deep breath, my heart fluttered for him for the first time. He pleaded for his life, which could be lost at any moment. Finally, we made this decision. He will stay on the ventilator no matter what's the cost. So, we kept him alive for ninety-six days, at the mercy of the machines.

Since Preman was hooked up to a ventilator, there was no point in me staying by his side the whole time. When I felt stifled in the hospital room, I would go outside for air and light. There is an old banyan tree on the east side of the hospital. There is a cemented platform around it. The tree provides soothing shade for the sick and those who accompany them. I spent my time there during the day when there was nothing to do.

The hustle and bustle of the hospital starts very early in the morning. Many people come and go every day. All the faces are puffy and sad. Some are crying, some are shedding tears inside. When I see the sorrow on their faces, I feel like my worries are light.

I have listened to some of their worries. Although I could not reassure all of them, I understood that I could reassure them, at least in a word.

Some needed medication for temporary relief. Some others needed food. Some ran back and forth for blood. I sat in the shade of the banyan tree and was busy.

I directed those who come to the hospital, who are sick and exhausted and do not know whom to meet or consult, and those who come to help their sick. So, I mingled with the hustle and bustle of the hospital.

Once I even went to Thiruvananthapuram Engineering College and AKG Centre to get blood for a patient who was near death due to bleeding.

From dawn till dusk, I had so much to do. Sometimes people would enquire about me when they could not find me under the banyan tree.

They would then ask for me in the nearby telephone booth. Manikantan, whose one leg was affected by polio, managed the phone box.

Sometimes I would call home to Guruvayoor from there and thus became familiar with him.

"Chechy, the old man from the twelfth ward asked for you."

"Chechy, Sister Sulochana has asked for you."

Thus, began a chain of services that included Manikantan.

"To do a service you do not have to come all the way to Calcutta. Look around you. There are so many unfortunate people waiting for a smile or a helping hand. We should not ignore them. "

The words I had heard from the Missionaries of Charity and Mother Teresa proved true.

Ninety-six days. Out of the futility of life, I dedicated myself to the needs of people without any support.

Those meaningful days reminded me not to waste my life in tears or remorseful recriminations.

I had a clear idea of my new path in life when I left for the house in Guruvayoor with Preman's lifeless body, as the hospital's life support machines were no longer taking care of him.

By the time the ambulance with Preman's motionless body reached the house in Guruvayoor, many friends and relatives had already gathered and Santhechy's loud crying was coming from the house into the courtyard.

All eyes fell on me.

I stepped out of the ambulance and entered the house with firm steps.

Paviyettan (Pavithran) and his friends performed his last rites.

A large crowd had gathered there, including his three wives and their relatives. Only Sharath is with me. The only proof that I lived with him.

It looked like it would be easy to push me away as I did not have a single relative to speak for me. Many started using sharp words to stifle any strength in me to fight for my rights.

But their hopes were dashed when they heard that Preman had drawn up a will. What Preman had kept for Umadevi, one of his wives, amazed not only them but me too.

He had not only deposited the house in Guruvayoor in my name but also a handsome amount of money.

This was my opportunity to stand up before those who sought me out and denigrated me with their words.

I stood proudly before those who wanted to reject Uma Devi, who did not have the legal rights of a wife.

I considered it more valuable to have asserted my rights as his wife than to gain possession of his property.

I survived the ordeal and proved myself pure.

I felt that I had taken a courage that was unknown to me until then.

A new light filled my eyes and cleared my mind.

With my head held high, I stood up and looked into the distance.

PART 3
YOUTH
Sky Without Limits

ONE

From strife to peace.

The turbulent phases in my life have come to an end. No longer held by the shackles of relationships, I had a clear idea of the path I wanted to take. A conviction that comes from oneself is the knowledge that there is nothing left to protest or control.

A hitherto unknown courage filled my words and actions. Paviyettan pointed this out to me as I went to get Preman's death certificate.

"You have changed a lot from the little girl who stood trembling before Preman. Where did you get all this courage?"

I held back my answer with a smile.

He knows my suffering very well. Because of his sincere love for his friend and his love for alcohol, he would have ignored it.

"When are you going to Delhi, Uma?"

Paviyettan tried to break my silence.

"The tenth," I said.

I had told Paviyettan and Dr. Neelakantan, who had treated Preman earlier, my decisions.

The doctor had encouraged me from the beginning.

"I told you about the new path in my life... Yesterday I mentioned it. "

If we had known about Preman's illness earlier, we could have treated it better. For several years it was thought to be the most common form of tuberculosis and he was taking medication for it. There must be many like him. A medical information centre will be useful to help those who do not know what diseases there are, how to treat them properly or where to go for treatment.

That was my aim.

Dr. Neelakantan was very enthusiastic about my plan.

"This is a good idea. It will help many people. Let me help you. "

The doctor's motivation gave me strength. Paviyettan was thinking in a different direction. He thought it was impossible for a simple girl.

"Uma, your idea is wonderful. But do not get involved in something where you would lose money. Always remember that there is no one to take care of you and your son."

That was his worry. It was a concern out of his brotherly love.

On the instructions of Dr. Neelakantan, I bought an HCL computer for one lakh rupees at a showroom in Thiruvananthapuram. I took a house on rent. Rajan, Harish and Sadanandan, who worked as assistants and drivers, joined me. I hired a data entry clerk.

Paviyettan started trusting me when he realized that things were happening faster and more systematically than he thought. One day when he came to the office, he asked me.

"Instead of just calling it the Medical Information Centre, we should give it a name. "

I replied to him that I would like that too.

"Shanthi,"

Without much hesitation, he gave a name. He smiled mysteriously.

"Shanthi Medical Information Centre, that's good."

Though I could guess the meaning of his smile, I hid it and indicated my favour to him.

Paviyettan looked me in the eye and repeated the name.

Shanthi (Peace): Not only for the sick, for you too."

Farewell to a life of discord, towards a life of perfect peace.

I just smiled.

In Delhi I was helped by a family I had known since my stay at Sree Chithra for the treatment of Preman. Viswettan and family. I went to Delhi because Viswettan told me he would help me collect information from the renowned hospitals there. We also prepared a brochure for the Shanthi Medical Information Centre there. Viswettan added a tagline to it.

"A place where you can get need-based information about specialties and super-specialties for treating various diseases."

I visited hospitals like All India Institute of Medical Sciences in Delhi, Dharmasala Metro Hospital, Kalidasa Hospital and Annapoorna Hospital and collected all the available information. The available brochures and information about the various departments and the services of the doctors were either written down or printed out and sent home by courier.

The data entry clerk's job was to enter this information into the computer. From Delhi, I also visited hospitals in Bombay, Kolkata, Hyderabad and Bangalore and collected relevant information.

There I became a member of the Connemara Public Library. I read books on various diseases. I could read almost ten books a day and could retain them in my memory all because of my good scanning memory.

I returned to Thrissur only after three months. By then, the information about almost all the important hospitals and special treatments were stored on Shanthi's computer.

As directed by Paviyettan, Shanthi Medical Information Centre was registered under the Charitable Society Act.

I was highly motivated. I was fully aware of the activities I was about to undertake. I got ready to work on it sleeplessly day and night.

On August 24, at the Thrissur Sahitya Akademi Hall, the Shanthi Medical Information Centre was officially established.

Bishop Kundukulam, Therambil Ramakrishnan, Paviyettan, his wife Kalamandalam Kshemavati, Kanayi Kunjiraman and some other friends were present at the inauguration. Bishop Kundukulam inaugurated Shanthi.

Nothing happened for almost a month.

No one understood anything about the Shanthi Medical Information Centre.

After a month, there was a news item about Shanthi on the front page of Mathrubhumi newspaper.

Without much delay, many calls and visitors came to Shanthi.

Subsequently, Shanthi grew busy with many free medical camps and other activities. The landlord panicked at the hustle and bustle. When he asked us to vacate the house, we moved to the house in Guruvayoor.

Slowly we reached a situation where there was no time when we were not busy. Medical camps, bedside help for people without any support, financial assistance projects — the activities increased.

I forgot about my past.

I lived alone in my new era.

TWO

It was two days before Vishu. The news of an accident came from Kodakara. Sujith, the eldest son of Ramachandran, a railway guard, was being treated at a private hospital in Thrissur for a head injury sustained when he fell from a mango tree. They were ready to take him elsewhere for expert help. So, they enquired about Shanthi. I called Dr. Ganesh from Kovai Medical College. He agreed to organize treatment facilities and so we started our journey with Sujith.

I had known Dr. Ganesh for a few years through Thankamani.

She worked as his secretary. Once we also took Preman there for treatment. When Shanthi began its activities, Dr Ganesh offered us his full support and cooperation. I was guided by this trust. His family too had high hopes. They believed that their son, now lying motionless, would regain consciousness.

But Sujith was already brain dead. When the neurosurgeon at Kovai Medical College confirmed this, his parents sat paralyzed.

The death of their son was a great shock to them. The mother sat motionless. She could not come out of the shock.

He was crying.

Dr. Ganesh called me into his room. Unusually, he started the conversation with a preamble.

"Uma, it is painful. But please listen carefully to what I am going to tell you now. "

I looked into his eyes. He looked serious.

"We could not save Sujith. But if we act now, we can help some other patients."I listened attentively. The doctor was talking about donating Sujith's eyes and kidneys.

This requires the consent of his parents. I have to take

this responsibility. How should I talk about this with the parents who have to cope with the painful loss of their son? I repeatedly told the doctor that I could not. But the doctor tried to encourage me.

"You are a social worker now. You need to be brave."

I have to be brave.

But how am I supposed to bring this to the father, who is sitting there drained and crying, and the mother, who is still in shock?

Because of the doctor's constant pressure, I went to them.

The woman was sitting, leaning on his shoulders, her eyes wide open. His eyes were blood red from crying. Very reluctantly, I told him the details. I expected him to explode. Because at that time, there was not much awareness of organ donation. But quite contrary to my expectations, he listened to me calmly.

"At least Sujith will continue to see this world through someone else's eyes. So ..."

I paused halfway through.

Silently he looked at his wife, who was leaning against his shoulder.

It looked as if she hadn't heard me at all.

He too said nothing for a short while.

I felt uncomfortable.

"Take your time and think. I said it because it's a good thing."

I just wanted to break out of the silence.

He looked at me and said,

"Do what it takes. "

His voice broke too.

My role wasn't over yet. Dr. Ganesh entrusted me with the task of getting the consent forms signed and informing her of further details.

Sujith's kidneys and eyes could be donated only after several complex procedures were completed. The delays in these procedures upset his parents.

As time progressed, he became very distressed. He lost his temper and even asked, " Will I get my son's body back?

It was already dark when we reached their house in Kodakara with the lifeless body of Sujith.

In the meantime, the relatives and the locals had heard about the organ donation. And that I was responsible for it.

People whispered among themselves as the body was put on the funeral pyre. Some even blamed me.

The pyre was ready. Someone was crying inside the house.

The people who had gathered watched with moist eyes. After the last ceremony, when the pyre was lit, I came out.

"Uma,"

I turned around when I heard someone calling out to me.

It was Sujith's father. His eyes red from crying. With quivering lips he said,

"Uma, thank you for everything."

"Let me tell you something else."

I looked at him.

"My son's body has gone under the knife because of your words."

"If your son is going through a similar ordeal, you must show the same sense of service."

There was a slight hint of sarcasm in his voice. It meant that words and actions diverge when people conduct their own affairs.

I walked away without words.

The smell of burning human flesh.

He dissolved into the air.

THREE

Shanthi had become a sanctuary for many. As we moved
Shanthi to the house at Guruvayoor, the hustle and bustle
increased. The activities didn't limit themselves to giving
information about hospitals and doctors. Along with the
patients, I too went to some hospitals. Some didn't have
anyone to assist them. Some didn't know what to do. I stood
by them, helping.

In addition to information sharing, Shanthi intervened
to make sure that the financial assistance from the
government reached eligible people.

As we made assistance from the Prime Minister's
Medical Assistance Fund available to many, the
undersecretary to the PM, P. G. George, contacted me.

Jovially he asked, if I had vowed to go from house to
house, making PM's fund available. He acknowledged the
vastness of Shanthi's work when he saw that applications
had started reaching them with Shanthi's cover letter, not
only from Kerala but from other states as well. He agreed
to meet me in person and do whatever was possible to help
us.

We had gone to the hospital in Coimbatore for the
diagnosis of the disease of Zainaba from Palakkad. Zainaba,
her twelve-year-old son, and I went. There were a lot of
patients in the waiting room.

We were to meet the nephrologist. The psychiatrist was
next door. As more seats were vacant there, we sat over
there.

I noticed the young man on my right. A dark-
complexioned youth, nearly twenty years old. As I saw him
sitting with his arm bent at the elbow, I asked him,

"*Ennappaa kaiyi?*" (Boy, what happened to your arm?)

He looked at me. He understood that I talked to him in
Tamil, taking him to be Tamilian.

"It's dialysis." he said. I was surprised.

"At this young age! Didn't you try a transplant?"

He glanced at me miserably. I talked to him about the possibility of a transplant.

"Kidney from your father or mother will suit you. Why didn't you consider it?"

"Both parents have passed on. Father had a heart attack. Two years ago, my mother too, due to kidney failure,"

He hung his face down.

I too fell silent, without words to comfort him. A patient came out of the doctor's room, another went in. We must wait a little longer.

I looked at the young man again. When I saw his sad face, my heart melted.

Suddenly I said to him.

"I have two kidneys. If it's all right with you, I can give you one."

He looked at me in amazement. He would have wondered why I was offering a body organ to an unknown person like him.

Doubt clouded his gaze. His gaze passed me and the name tag of the doctor we were sitting at.

He acknowledged it.

A patient who came to see the psychiatrist. A smile tugged at his lips. He looked at me from head to toe and murmured to his companion.

"She looks normal. But she's crazy."

The other huffed.

"We had a serious talk. At the end she said she would donate a kidney to me."

As they talked, they laughed.

The person accompanying him looked at me kindly. I stood up, went to him and introduced myself.

"I am not crazy. I was serious about it. Do not worry about it. Just think of me as your elder sister."

His eyes welled up.

I saw Thambikuttan in him. Thambikuttan who followed me everywhere like a tail. After being an orphan, he had thrown his life into disarray, I could not control him. He had become very stubborn in his life.

Whenever I tried to meet him, he would avoid me. It could

be that he thought I was an obstacle on the path of pleasure he had chosen for himself. Still...

I looked into Salil's eyes. He stood there, confused.

I went in with them to meet the doctor.

I also communicated my decision to the doctor. But when he mentioned that we should consider transplantation only after six to seven months of dialysis, I started doubting its possibilities.

I told him about it too.

So, we went to see Dr. Ganesh at Kovai Medical College.

The doctor was shocked at my decision.

He discouraged me.

"Uma, I know you are committed to the society. But this has gone too far."

He scolded me and told me not to play with my life in the name of social service. I was not ready to change my decision. I asked the doctor an important question.

"Will anything happen to me if I donate a kidney?"

He replied that nothing would happen.

But he did not understand the logic of putting an organ from someone he knew well into the body of someone he did not know. That was the reason for his refusal.

I stood firm on my decision. When I threatened that I would find another hospital if he did not make the necessary arrangements, the doctor relented. Though Thankamani resisted initially, she later decided to stand by me. She was always on my side, come what may.

He was called Salil.

Unnikrishnan, alias Salil, is the son of Kottappadi Vadakkeppuraykkal Balakrishnan and Valsala. Salil, who worked as a car consultant in Tirupur, was keeping himself alive with the help of dialysis for the past six months.

Doctors have told them that transplantation is possible only if they find a kidney from someone with blood group O-negative. Although Salil, whose parents passed away, approached many relatives, it was in vain. At that time, without any prior acquaintance, I had approached him and offered him my kidney.

On the instructions of Dr. Ganesh, the hospital initiated the procedure for kidney donation.

My blood group was O-positive. This cleared the first hurdle. Both matched. The doctors tested me and gave their okay.

As part of the kidney donation procedure, a meeting was held with the Medical Council. The medical director was Dr. Balasubramaniam.

At first, he couldn't believe it. That day Sharath was also with me. A seven-year-old, he sat staring ahead, with no idea of what his mother would do.

The doctor looked at him and me alternately and asked

"Uma is still very young. Did you agree to the donation voluntarily aware of all the consequences?"

I nodded in agreement.

At that time organ donation wasn't so widespread even after death. At that time, I was ready to donate an organ to an unknown person. He looked me in the eye and asked again.

"Aren't you afraid that something unfortunate might happen to you during the operation to remove your kidney?"

As the doctor asked this question, I looked at Sharath. His gaze was fixed on the paperweight on the table. While his eyes caught the colourful views in the glass, he didn't notice my gaze or the seriousness of the question the doctor was asking.

I put my arm on his shoulder and answered the doctor.

"If there is a mishap, you can take both kidneys, eyes and any other organs that are useful to others."

The doctor didn't ask any more questions. I smiled at Sharath. Not knowing much, he too smiled. They fixed the date of the operation. When I said that I wouldn't be with him for a few days, he asked me something more.

A Shakthiman costume.

"When Amma comes, please bring it for me."

As he babbled, I couldn't help laughing.

"The son who sold his mother's kidney for the Shakthiman dress."

I kissed him on the cheek.

The operation was performed by a team of doctors led by Dr. Devadas Madhavan and Dr. Vivek Pathak.

Salil and I were lying on adjacent beds.

Salil's sister was with him.

In the office we said Thankamani was being operated on. So, there were no questions.

Salil's face was shadowed with fear.

Salil had instructed his sister to take care of Sharath in case any mishap happened to me during the operation.

The kidney on my right side became Salil's life-saving kidney.

As we retrieved his life, which he had almost lost the day after the operation, with tears in his eyes, Salil came to my bedside in a wheelchair and said to me,

"Chechy, you are my God, the God who gave me life."

Wincing in pain, I tried to smile but could not. I had thirty-two sutures on my stomach. It was a huge wound sewn together.

It took many days for the wound to heal. The pain also subsided.

Headlines appeared in the daily newspapers praising the donation of kidneys to an unknown person, and the number of people visiting Shanthi and enquiring about donating a

kidney increased. The phone calls were also about kidneys.

Once, a mother tearfully asked.

"Save my son; give me a kidney."

I tried to convince her of my helplessness.

"I have already donated a kidney. We cannot transplant a kidney from everyone. You have to find a suitable kidney. "

She was not ready to listen to me. She whimpered loudly.

"I just need one. I want my son to survive too. "

There is a high level of ignorance about kidney disease and organ donation. Another patient asked on another occasion

"If I get a kidney from my old mother, will I die when she dies?"

Shanthi strove to bridge the gap between this kind of ignorance and clear knowledge about organ donation.

To the mother who refused to donate a kidney to her only son and the wife who refused to donate a kidney to her husband, I can boldly say,

"There is no problem. You may courageously donate kidneys."

In the past, relatives used to scoff.

"It is easy to preach. Practicing is difficult. "

But now I can tell them.

No one would sneer.

When he returned to his normal life after the transplant, he called every day from Tirupur.

He was worried about how he was going to repay me.

Once he said in a hoarse voice,

"I feel grateful and in debt. Who in this world would be willing to do that? To give back one's life..."

Now Salil is involved in Shanthi's activities in Guruvayoor.

Salil came as a stranger and became a brother, by blood. He is the twin brother I have gained in this life.

FOUR

Orphanhood. Only those who have experienced it, understand its agony. Although my parents were still alive, I had to live like an orphan at a certain stage of my life. The people who supported me in such situations were not blood relatives. If you belong to the hearts whose sources of love surpass those of blood relations and do not dry up, you will not feel like an orphan. That is my experience.

When I saw Mariyappan, he was very ill. The twenty-two-year-old was suffering from kidney disease. Srinivasan and his wife Ajitha from Guruvayoor, took Mariyappan to Shanthi as the doctors advised a kidney transplant to save his life.

I too felt pained when I saw his tired body and frail face. I heard his story. Mariyappan is the son of Selvaraj and Pappathi from Ambattur, Chennai. A group of child traffickers brought him and his sister Kaliyammal to Kerala. He was seven years old then. Kaliyammal was taken to the Kothamangalam area. Mariyappan was sold to a family in the Mattom area near Guruvayoor. Mariyappan was in poor health and unable to do the heavy work he was made to do; he was thrown out on the streets. He fed himself on the food waste thrown away by the hotels nearby. He spent his days drinking water from the taps on the street and sleeping on the verandas of shops. Kulangara Srinivasan from Mallipparambu, Guruvayoor, took him home from there. Then Mariyappan fell ill with a severe skin infection. Mariyappan became the son of Srinivasan and his wife, who had two daughters. They named him Babu.

They taught him to read and write.

Even as his life went on happily, the urge to meet his real parents did not subside. It became even stronger as his kidney disease progressed.

Srinivasan and his wife did not reject him even when they came to know about the severity of his kidney disease. They sold their two cows, which were their main source of income, and treated him. It was only when the doctors suggested a kidney transplant that they sought help from Shanthi.

At Shanthi, we organized free dialysis for him. His treatment progressed. On the other hand, they also made efforts to find a suitable kidney for him.

One day, very reluctantly, he asked me.

"Ma'am, I would like to meet my father and mother. Would you help me with that?"

I patted him on the shoulder to reassure him.

I assured that we would try. I sought help from my journalist friends in Tamil Nadu. He also posted his story on Facebook groups.

Finally,

In Ambattur, we found Mariyappan's family.

Mother Pappathi, stepfather Chandran and younger sister Jayalakshmi came and identified him. They lived with him for almost three months. Srinivasan's family thought that their presence would give some relief to Mariyappan.

In the meantime, I worked hard to get kidneys for him.

When we found his mother, things became easier. We found that Pappathi's kidney matched Mariyappan's kidney.

But things were not as easy as we thought. They insisted on taking him to Ambattur and treating him there. Pappathi, who was originally willing to donate a kidney, changed her mind. They ignored our protests and took Mariyappan to Ambattur.

As his kidney disease was advanced, regular dialysis was very important for him. Mariyappan's family, already plagued by poverty, did not seriously consider this. The more his disease progressed, the more they rejected him.

Abandoned even by his mother, he returned to Shanthi within four days. With his body swollen and bloated, he burst into tears in front of me.

Even I was at a loss for words.

With dialysis, he overcame the critical situation.

We accommodated him at the Snehalaya in Mundathikkodu.

But the disease ate away at his body.

He was again admitted in a very critical condition.

In the emergency ward of Thrissur Metropolitan Hospital.

Srinivasan and his family waited outside with prayers and vows.

All our loving efforts were in vain and Mariyappan died.

We informed his relatives. But no one came to collect the body.

I detested cremating him as a pauper. I informed Sharath.

After allowing a public viewing at the Shanthi premises, Sharath performed the last rites.

Srinivasan and his family, along with the Shanthi staff, attended the rituals and bid him farewell.

With quivering lips, Sharath repeated the priest's chants.

"*Mama sahodara Mariyappa...* (my brother Mariyappa...) Hearing him chant this, those gathered burst into tears.

Mariyappan left this world with many relatives, proving that relationships built on love are stronger than those created by birth.

FIVE

The trail of scenes from my past are always with me. Many of them I would not like to relive.

We cannot go back in time.

If I could, I could have avoided some events.

Some of the scenes that I detest would then have disappeared from my life.

I would like to believe that what has happened and what will happen is inevitable.

Life includes happiness, sadness and also wounds.

Often, I wanted to talk, to open up to someone and ease my sorrow. But with whom?

When life stood before me like a big question mark, I talked to the walls. My sorrow, my worries, my longings — they heard all that. Maybe that's why every event from my past is anchored in me like an image.

In those days when I sat numb, not knowing what to do, someone whispered from within me.

"Hopes are our assets. Do not lose them."

The past is a reality.

I must accept it for what it is.

The lack of love, the insults or the ridicule from my past no

longer haunt me. The pain they caused no longer hurts.

I have enclosed my past within four walls.

Today, the world outside those walls is my life.

My firm and resolute steps led me down a difficult path, from a time of perplexity when I had no solid ground under my feet and did not even know where to rest my head.

www.ingramcontent.com/pod-product-compliance
Lightning Source LLC
Chambersburg PA
CBHW020551020726
47494CB00006B/2021

* 9 781739 215996 *